Faithful, But Not Famous

"You must know more of Claude Leclerc's ways
and doings than this maiden can."

EMMA LESLIE CHURCH HISTORY SERIES

Faithful, But Not Famous

A Tale of the French Reformation

BY

EMMA LESLIE

Illustrated by
W. Q.

Salem Ridge Press
Emmaus, Pennsylvania

Originally Published
1872
The Religious Tract Society

Republished 2009
Salem Ridge Press LLC
4263 Salem Drive
Emmaus, Pennsylvania 18049

www.salemridgepress.com

Hardcover ISBN: 978-1-934671-29-0
Softcover   ISBN: 978-1-934671-30-6

PUBLISHER'S NOTE

When we think of the Reformation there are names that stand out, like Wycliffe, Luther and Calvin. Two that usually do not come to mind are Dr. Lefèvre and Guillaume Farel, yet God in His wisdom allowed them be among the first to spread the light in a time of great darkness. As they earnestly searched the Scriptures and sought the Lord, they were used by Him to bring the good news of salvation to thousands and to begin the Reformation in France.

Like Dr. Lefèvre and Guillaume Farel, each of us has been given a job to do by the Lord, and like them we each have the opportunity to remain faithful, even though we may never be famous.

Daniel Mills

June, 2009

PREFACE TO THE 1872 EDITION

In the following pages an attempt is made to narrate, in a popular form, the origin and early progress of Protestantism in France. The main events and the principal characters of the story are strictly historical. The minor details have been introduced, not merely for the sake of effect, but with the object of presenting a true and faithful picture of the manners, customs, and state of feeling in France at the time. The period covered by our story does not extend beyond the dawn of the Reformation. It stops short of the era of relentless persecution.

It will thus be seen how much there was in the state of the public mind to encourage the enthusiastic hopes of Lefèvre, Farel, and their associates, on the one hand; and yet how great were the difficulties with which they had to contend, on the other. At the outset it appeared as though France was so thoroughly prepared to receive the Gospel, and the early progress of evangelical doctrine was so rapid, that its speedy victory over papal error was confidently expected. No one could have anticipated the almost total extinction of the light of truth in the country which so eagerly welcomed it, and in which, indeed, it was first kindled.

1872 PREFACE

D'Aubigné shows that the doctrine of justification by faith alone was preached by Lefèvre at a time when Luther was yet struggling with conviction, and Zwingle was a devoted servant of the Papacy.

Emma Leslie

HISTORICAL NOTES

Several important historical figures from the fifteenth and sixteenth centuries A.D. are mentioned in *Faithful, But Not Famous.* Here is a brief summary of some of these people:

Louisa of Savoy: Born in A.D. 1476, Louisa was the oldest daughter of Philip II, Duke of Savoy. At the age of eleven, Louisa was married to Count Charles of Orleans. Four year later their first child, Marguerite, was born, followed two years later by a son, Francis. Widowed at the age of nineteen, Louisa moved her family to the court of King Louis XII of France and arranged for the marriage of Francis to Louis' daughter, Claude. Following Francis' coronation in A.D. 1515, Louisa continued to have a powerful influence in her son's life until her death in A.D. 1531.

Francis I: As the nearest male relative of Louis XII, Francis was already heir to the French throne when he married Louis' daughter, Claude, in A.D. 1514. Following Louis' death in A.D. 1515, Francis was crowned King of France. Through the influence of his sister, Marguerite, Francis tolerated and protected the reformers for a time, but towards the end of his reign he mercilessly persecuted them.

HISTORICAL NOTES

Marguerite of Navarre: Instructed along with her brother, Francis, Marguerite became one of the most educated women of her time. In A.D. 1509, at the age of seventeen, Marguerite was married to Charles IV, Duke of Alençon. Marguerite was strongly influenced in her religious beliefs by her correspondence with William Briçonnet, Bishop of Meaux. Although she never officially joined the Reformation, she sought to protect the reformers through her great influence with her brother, the king. Following the death of her husband in A.D. 1525, Marguerite was married to King Henry II of Navarre.

William Briçonnet: As bishop of the City of Meaux near Paris, William Briçonnet was at first a powerful force for reform from within the Church. Over time, however, the charges of heresy brought against him and against his friends, including Dr. Lefèvre and Guillaume Farel, took their toll and he abandoned his attempts at reform.

Dr. Lefèvre of Etaples: Born in northern France in A.D. 1455, Dr. Lefèvre traveled widely before arriving at the Sorbonne University in Paris. By A.D. 1493, Dr. Lefèvre was a Doctor of Divinity and a professor at the University. In the early 1500's, Dr. Lefèvre began work on an extensive project to collect and publish the legends of the saints. After publishing two volumes, however, he abandoned the work and instead began to study the Scriptures and write commentaries. In A.D. 1511, Dr. Lefèvre became the first preacher of the Reformation to teach the doctrine of justification by faith. Constantly accused of heresy, Dr. Lefèvre was protected on many occasions by Francis I and Marguerite. One of Dr. Lefèvre's greatest achievements was the translation of the Bible into French. At last, to escape persecution, Dr. Lefèvre fled France to the protection of Marguerite in Navarre, where he died in A.D. 1536.

Guillaume Farel: Born in A.D. 1489 in southern France, Guillaume Farel came to Paris in A.D. 1510 and soon became a student of Dr. Lefèvre's. Through his own study of the Bible, Farel became convinced of the truth of the gospel as taught by Dr. Lefèvre. Later, because of intense persecution, Farel traveled first to Meaux and then back to his native Dauphiny, spreading the gospel throughout the region. In A.D. 1524, Farel fled France for Switzerland where he worked closely with John Calvin in Geneva for many years.

In the late sixth century A.D., Pope Gregory I began to preach the doctrine of **purgatory**. He proposed it as a place where those who have died could pay for the sins that they committed during their lives before going to heaven, however this doctrine is completely contrary to salvation by grace.

HISTORICAL NOTES

Upon his election as pope in A.D. 1503, Julius II promised to hold a council to discuss possible reforms within the Church, however he avoided actually calling the council for many years. When the **Lateran Council** was finally held in A.D. 1512, it was concluded that little reform was needed.

In A.D. 1516, Francis I and Pope Leo X reached an agreement called the **Concordat of Bologna**. This agreement allowed the pope to collect all of the revenue from the Church in France while giving Francis the authority to appoint all of the church officials. The Concordat was fiercely opposed by the bishops, priests and monks because it gave the king complete control of the French Church.

IMPORTANT DATES

A.D.

1510 Guillaume Farel arrives in Paris as a student

1511 Dr. Lefèvre preaches justification by faith

1515 Francis I crowned King of France

1516 Briçonnet appointed Bishop of Meaux

1517 Martin Luther writes his *Ninety-five Theses*

1522 Lefèvre completes his French New Testament

1524 Farel flees France for Switzerland

1530 Lefèvre's complete French Bible published

1531 Lefèvre flees France for Navarre

CONTENTS

ILLUSTRATIONS

Faithful, But Not Famous

Faithful, But Not Famous

Chapter I

The Armorer of the Petit Pont

SPRING sunshine was just peeping through the vine and olive leaves in the gardens of Dauphiny when a stout, rosy-faced peasant lad set forth from his native village with a small bundle slung over his shoulder, and a stout stick in his hand. By his side walked an elderly careworn woman; but they had not got far beyond the village before the youth stopped.

"You must go back now, Mother, or you will be tired," he said. But though he begged his mother to return, he did not seem disposed to go on.

"You must not linger, Claude," said the woman, a little sternly; "it is a weary march to Paris, and you will be some days on the road."

"I wish I were not going," said the youth. "I have no wish to become a priest; I would rather stay and help you work in the vineyard."

His mother looked displeased. "Never say that again, Claude," she said; "it is an honor to enter the service of the Church, and it ought to be enough for you that Father Antoine and I both wish it."

It was not enough for the youth, apparently, for he still looked discontented and unhappy. "I would rather stay and work for you and Margot and Fanchon, than go to this school of St. Germain l'Auxerrois. I ought to stay and work for you," he added, almost passionately, "for you are a widow, and have no other son that can help you."

"Hush, hush, Claude, you must be content to do as the holy father bids you. It would be wrong—wicked—to disobey his commands, and the terrible curse of the Church would fall upon you if you did;" and the poor woman fairly trembled with terror as she spoke.

But the boy still looked unconvinced and unsatisfied. He felt very little reverence for the Church or the priests either. He had been indifferent until lately, merely going to mass and confession to

please his mother; but indifference was giving
place to positive hatred, now that he was forced
to leave home and friends, and go into a world of
strangers at the bidding of the priest. This, too,
was increased by the thought of what his mother
would suffer, but she had little fear.

"I can work," she said, "and so can Margot;
and, if sickness comes, our noble and kind friend,
Madame Farel, will help us. You know Guillaume
Farel said so when he heard you were to become
a priest."

"But Guillaume Farel will be going to Paris himself very soon," said Claude, still in the same discontented tone.

"But his family will not; and let this content you,
my son, that it is needful for you to go to Paris."
And having said this she once more bade him fare-
well, and resolutely turned back, though it cost her
heart a pang to do this, and leave him standing in
the road.

How much it cost his mother to part with him
Claude did not know. He believed that the priest
had worked upon her superstitious fears, to induce
her to send him from home, and devote him to the
service of the Church; but of the agony it cost her,
he knew nothing.

Nor did he know fully what had caused this
decision. Only a few fragments had reached his
ears. The valleys of Dauphiny are so near those
of the Waldenses, that some rays of religious light

INDUCE: *lead*

continually penetrated from one to the other. Claude's father had received a measure of saving truth. Hence he became an object of suspicion and aversion to the priests of the districts in which he lived; and on his death, Father Antoine came to the conclusion that the best way to eradicate the taint of heresy from the family would be to compel the widow to dedicate her only son to the Church. He would thus prove his zeal to his ecclesiastical superiors, and check the further spread of the hated doctrines in the village.

Claude had now reached the age at which he must begin his studies for the priesthood; and the widow was compelled to give up her son in fulfillment of the vow she had made, in the hope of procuring the deliverance of her husband's soul from purgatory.

After they had parted the youth stood for awhile watching his mother's receding figure as she passed up the road, and wondering when he should see his native village again. Not for many years, he feared; for Father Antoine had told him he must not return until he had cast out the love of mother and sisters from his heart—that henceforth his whole love and life must be given to the Church.

Slowly and sadly he turned away as the last glimpse of his mother was lost, and a bitter feeling arose in his heart against the Church and priests alike.

ERADICATE: *completely remove*
HERESY: *views that go against accepted beliefs*
ECCLESIASTICAL: *church*

Although Paris, in the year 1510, was already re-nowned for her patronage of learning, and for all the latest improvements of the age, the roads from the south of France to the capital were little better than mule tracts and bridle paths, often leading through miles of forest infested with wild boars and wolves, and scarcely less savage bands of rob-bers.

Of the latter, however, Claude had little to fear, for he had nothing to lose; but the bad state of the roads, and the care required in passing through the forests, made his progress very slow and te-dious, and he was many days upon the journey.

But Claude's long march came to an end at last, and the gate of Paris was gained. He was just in time to enter before the gate closed for the night. Faint, weary, and footsore, he made his way through the ville or town, as one-third of Paris was called, by the Rue St. Jacques to the shop-crowded Petit Pont, one of the bridges over the Seine, unit-ing the island—the original city of Paris—to its suburb, the ville.

At the shop of an armorer, the shutters of which were not yet closed, he stopped to inquire his way to Pont Nôtre Dame, for he had heard that the monastery at which he was to deliver his letter was not far from this bridge. The young girl who came forward as he went in, glanced at his travel-stained clothes, and pale, weary face, as she said, "You must be a stranger in Paris not to know that the

Pont Nôtre Dame is in a straight line from here."

"I am a stranger," said Claude, glancing curiously at the brightly gleaming pieces of armor and coats of mail hanging round.

The girl looked at him again, and then said, "Wait a minute until I fetch my mother," and darted away into a room at the back of the shop. In a minute or two she returned, followed by a kindly-looking matron, who, glancing at Claude's tired look, said, "You cannot walk further tonight."

"Nay, I am not so tired but I can walk a little farther," said Claude; but his looks belied his words.

"Thou art from the country, I perceive," said the armorer's wife.

"Yes, I am from the province of Dauphiny," said Claude. "I have come to your school of St. Germain l'Auxerrois."

"There, Mother, did I not say he was a poor scholar," whispered the girl; "and you know my father always likes to help them if he can."

The matron held up her finger warningly. "Where do you lodge tonight?" she asked.

"I know not, unless I find shelter at the monastery," said Claude.

"The brothers of St. Germain l'Auxerrois are but poor men themselves," said the armorer's wife. "I advise you to tarry here. All poor scholars are welcome to what we have to give—a morsel of bread and a shelter for the night," she added, in a pleasant voice.

BELIED: *contradicted*

Claude was anxious to reach the monastery as soon as possible, but he did not like to refuse the proffered kindness; and it was well he did not, for he was far more exhausted than he thought. No sooner had the need for exertion ceased than his strength gave way, and he had scarcely uttered his thanks before he fell fainting on the floor.

"Run, Babette, and fetch some water, and get me some burnt feathers," said the matron, raising Claude's head.

"Oh, Mother, is he dead?" asked the girl in a frightened whisper.

"No, no; he is only overcome with weariness and hunger, perhaps. Poor boy, he looks very ill, and not fit for the hard life of a poor scholar."

It was some time before Claude recovered. Warm cordials had been given him, and he was lying on a bed in a little room at the side of the shop—a little slip that seemed to have been portioned off from its width, and used as a storeroom for old armor. Rusty poniards, chain coats, breastplates and *espadons*, or two-edged swords, were hung round the walls, or piled in the corners. But Claude did not see these at once, for a kind, motherly face was bending over him, and he heard a gentle voice say, "Is he better, Mother?" and then the door opened, and a tall, benevolent-looking man came in, and Babette exclaimed, "Father, here is a poor scholar almost dying from his long walk from Dauphiny."

PROFFERED: *offered*
PONIARDS: *daggers*

"From Dauphiny," repeated the armorer; "why, surely all the lads are coming from Dauphiny to our Sorbonne."

"Why?" asked Babette, and her mother looked the same question as she again put the cordial to Claude's lips.

"Well, I have been to see Maître Thibauld in the Rue St. Denis, and he tells me a young noble from Dauphiny, Monseigneur Farel, arrived there this afternoon, and craved a lodging."

"And he has come to our far-famed Sorbonne," said the matron, with a touch of pride.

"Yes, our little doctor of Etaples is the great attraction, as thou knowest," said the armorer.

"What other news hast thou heard tonight?" asked his wife, without noticing how her patient had started at the name of Farel.

"Well, something that will stir all Paris, and the Sorbonne, too, methinks," answered the armorer. "Thou heardest that my former customer, Monsieur Bodæus, had suddenly given up hawks and dogs, tilting and tournaments, to apply himself to study."

"Ah! a good customer we have lost in him," sighed the matron; "for he always paid his debts right honestly, although he lived so riotously. But what of him?" she asked; "I heard that he was as earnest now in the pursuit of learning as he had formerly been in the pursuit of pleasure."

"Ah! but the learning is not of the right sort according to our Sorbonne. The learned physician,

TILTING: *jousting*

Cop, and Monsieur Vatable, with Bodæus, have set themselves to the study of Greek and Hebrew, which the Sorbonne has declared to be deadly heresy."

"Heresy?" repeated his wife. The word had not grown to be a terror then, and she scarcely knew its meaning.

"Yes, the learned professors declare that the study of these languages will lead men to forsake the teaching of our holy mother Church, and blaspheme the name of the ever-blessed Virgin."

The matron looked shocked. "Why, there must be witchcraft in it," she said; "why do not the Sorbonne burn all the books?"

"They would if they could; but the Jews, as thou knowest, are everywhere, and the Hebrew is their native language—so it cannot be done."

"But the Sorbonne will prevent them from learning this dreadful language," said Babette.

"They will if they can," replied her father; "but the Sorbonne and our bishop are not agreed about this thing. He and Monsieur Ruzé, the lieutenant of the city, take the part of these students against the Sorbonne; and it is said that the king's niece and nephew, Marguerite and Francis of Valois, lean towards them, too."

"And our little learned doctor of Etaples, what of him?" asked the matron.

"Oh, thou knowest he is a most learned man, as well as a devout Catholic; and so he would see but little danger in these studies."

This pleasant gossip was here interrupted by the entrance of a customer whom the apprentice could not serve; and by the time Frollo had suited him, and the shop been shut up, Claude had so far recovered, that Babette and her mother went to have their own supper, leaving him to wonder how Guillaume Farel had managed to reach Paris so soon. For Farel was his own near neighbor in Dauphiny, they had played together as children; and Claude knew that he had left home for Paris some time after he himself had started.

He had not paid much heed to the rest of the gossip, beyond remembering the name of the learned professor, Dr. Lefèvre of Etaples. In the midst of conjectures about when he should see Guillaume Farel, he fell asleep.

The ringing and clattering of the armorer and his apprentice at their work awoke Claude the next morning, and he got up feeling greatly refreshed, but still very weak. When he had partaken of some breakfast which his kind host insisted upon his eating, he set off in search of the far-famed school of St. Germain l'Auxerrois. He had little difficulty in finding it; and the monk to whom his letter was addressed, having charge of the school, he had no difficulty in gaining admission as a day scholar; but beyond this, Brother Clement could not help him.

Claude looked dismayed. He had not thought to ask Father Antoine whether all his wants would be supplied as soon as he reached Paris—he had taken it for granted that it would be so—and he could only look at the monk in blank amazement when he said: "My son, we can give the bread of knowledge here; but we are too poor to do more than that."

"But what am I to do then?" faltered Claude; "I am very poor; my mother is a widow."

"But you wish to become a priest, and—"

"Father Antoine commanded me to come here," interrupted Claude, quickly.

The monk waved his hand and frowned. "The Church has decreed that you shall serve her, and you must not rebel. The discipline is doubtless needful—the humility and poverty to be borne as a poor scholar;" and without another word, the monk turned away, and Claude was summoned to take his place in the class appointed. At dinner-time most of the scholars went home, and the monks retired to the monastery; but there was another scholar seemingly as poor as Claude himself, and they both drew near to the fire, which was burning brightly on the wide hearth.

"You are not going home," said the other, looking up from the volume he was reading, and speaking in a courteous tone.

"I have no home in Paris," said Claude, with a deep sigh, as he thought of the little cottage so many leagues away.

"Neither have I," returned his companion; "so that in that we are alike. We are both poor scholars."

"I am poor enough," said Claude, bitterly; "for I know not where to get a shelter at night, or how I am to earn my living and attend the school."

"And the school you must attend," said the other, decisively.

Claude nodded. "You are very fond of learning," he said, noticing the book.

"Yes, very. I forget that I have no dinner when I have a book like this," and he looked fondly at the volume he held in his hand.

Claude did not ask what it was. He cared more for his dinner just now, and said rather impatiently, "Well, can you tell me how I am to get something to eat, for I am very hungry."

"Can you sing?" asked his companion.

"I used to sing in the choir at home," replied Claude.

"Then you can sing in the streets here," said the other; "when singing fails, you will have to depend upon charity, as many other poor scholars do."

Claude shrugged his shoulders. This was not at all to his liking. The young peasant who had been used to honest labor, could not descend to be a beggar at once. "I can work," he said, "and I will do so;" and he left the schoolroom at once to make inquiries in the neighborhood for some work that he could do between school hours.

When the monastery bell rang for the scholars to reassemble, Claude crept back to his place in the class, weary, hungry, and thoroughly dispirited; for no one would employ him, and one or two had even laughed at his application.

When afternoon school was over, all were compelled to leave the shelter of the schoolroom; and Claude, with the other poor scholar, shrank behind their more fortunate companions, and were thus thrown together again.

"Come with me tonight, and I will help you if I can," he whispered to Claude.

The poor boy was growing almost desperate, and he knew his companion must be very hungry, for he had been at school all day without having anything to eat; but at the sound of the *vesper* bell he turned into one of the neighboring churches, and remained until the service was over, Claude, meanwhile, growing very impatient. "I don't believe in it; I don't believe in anything; I don't mean to go to school anymore," he said, as they were leaving.

The other looked shocked. "Hush! hush! you must not talk in that way," he said, reprovingly. "You will feel better tomorrow; you are hungry, and cold, and tired now." He had a little money in his pocket—enough to buy himself a meal, and this he cheerfully shared with Claude; and then they went out in search of a sheltered corner where they could stand and sing.

No one interrupted them. It was so usual for poor peasant lads who had a taste for learning, and came to Paris penniless, for the sake of attending one of the schools, to get their living in this way, that it was hardly looked upon as a disgrace, and

VESPER BELL: *bell for evening prayers*

many who did not care for the singing gave the boys small coins.

After singing for about an hour at this corner, Claude proposed that they should go somewhere else.

"We shall not get much more tonight," said Jacques, "unless we get asked into some of the large houses."

"Do you ever go to the Rue St. Denis?" asked Claude, thinking of his friend Guillaume Farel. He remembered the name of the street where he lived, and asked where it was.

"The Rue St. Denis, oh, we will go there," said Jacques. "We are lucky tonight," he said, as he counted over his money by the light of the flaring street torches; "we have enough to pay for a lodging, and get some breakfast in the morning—the sweet Mother of mercy has heard my prayer." He bowed and crossed himself as he passed one of her shrines at the same moment; but Claude turned away: he was weary and hungry and homesick.

Claude had now more leisure to look about him, and notice the splendid buildings of the city. To a country lad who had never seen a town until within the last few weeks, the sight of so many magnificent houses, churches, abbeys, and monasteries, seemed almost bewildering. They were in the University suburb where these abounded, and where the Sorbonne—half-monastery, half-college—ruled as the king did in the city proper —the island city which the old chronicler[1] speaks

---

[1] French historian Henri Sauval (1623-1676)
GAY: *bright and cheerful*

of as "like a great ship sunk in the mud, and run aground lengthwise in the stream about the middle of the Seine." The river was sparkling, as though it had caught and imprisoned a thousand stars; for lights were gleaming from the windows of the houses on the different bridges, making it look almost as gay as modern Paris, with its myriad jets of gas, although gas had not then been heard of.

For our two poor scholars who could not afford to buy a torch, the narrow winding streets were very dark and very perplexing too; although Jacques thought he had mastered all its intricacies. Claude followed him, wondering when they should reach the Rue St. Denis. Not that he had any intention of seeking assistance from Guillaume Farel—he had quite made up his mind not to do that, but he would like to see him as he passed. Thinking of Guillaume Farel, he had quite forgotten that Jacques had told him not to lose sight of him in going round the corners of streets; and now, as he looked up, he saw nothing of his companion. He ran forward a few steps, but was almost knocked down by coming in contact with the buttress of one of the houses; and when he had recovered from this blow, Jacques was still nowhere to be seen.

In vain Claude called him by name, and sang the hymn to the Virgin which Jacques had told him was his favorite. No one came in answer to his calling or singing; and at last he had to give himself up to the thought that he was lost in the streets of Paris.

JETS OF GAS: *gas lamps*
BUTTRESS: *a stone support for a wall*

Chapter II

Poor Scholars of Paris

How long he had been walking, or how he got there, Claude never knew; but just as he thought he had succeeded in finding the Rue St. Denis, he saw the armorer's shop where he had lodged the night before. Frollo, standing at the door to see that his apprentice put up the shutters properly, saw the poor scholar, and held out his hand in pleasant welcome. Claude could not but feel glad when he was invited in to supper, and to occupy the little lumber room again, for he knew not where to seek Jacques now; and yet he looked somewhat abashed as he went to where Babette and her mother were sitting busy with their distaffs, for he did not like to be thought a beggar.

"I was looking for the Rue St. Denis," he said. "Another poor scholar has been with me this evening, and we have been singing, and were going to the Rue St. Denis to do so again, when I lost him, and lost my way."

ABASHED: *ashamed or embarrassed*
DISTAFFS: *staffs used in spinning wool or flax*

"Had you no torch?" asked Babette; but her mother looked at her reprovingly for speaking before her father or herself; and Claude noticing her confusion, and how she was tangling her threads of flax, hastened to ask Frollo the way to the Rue St. Denis, that Babette might escape further notice.

The girl lifted her head, and looked gratefully at Claude in a minute or two, and he thought, "How much she is like my sister Margot!"

Babette did not venture to speak again, for her father was telling Claude what wonders the new invention of printing was likely to effect. "Why, even poor burgher-folk like me will be able to buy a book now," he said.

"Nay, nay, 'tis nothing to rejoice at," quickly interrupted his wife; "'tis Satan's invention, this printing; and religion will soon be at an end through the evil books that make a mock of all the holy mysteries and priests and monks."

"Aye, but 'tis not the fault of the books, but the priests and monks whose evil lives they expose," replied her husband.

"I should like to see some of these books," said Claude, eagerly.

Frollo laughed. "They will not give you these at the school of St. Germain l'Auxerrois," he said.

"Nay, nay, the lad does not want them," said Madame, trying to check her husband's flow of talk in this direction.

BURGHER-FOLK: *inhabitants of a borough or town*

"'Twill do him no harm, I trow, to look at the fox's head beneath the monk's cowl," said Frollo; "for we know they are foxes, wolves, and swine, these holy fathers who are set to be our guides."

"Nay, nay, talk not so before the lad," said Madame; "if we in Paris are forced to know such things, it is not seemly that our peasant lads should."

"Then they must not come to Paris," said her husband, "for there is never a day but some scandalous tale is told of their doings in the city, and 'tis a wonder, if there is a God, that He doesn't sweep them off the earth."

Madame would not let her husband say any more, but begged him to fetch up the tankard of wine, while she set out Claude's supper. But, although nothing more was said, Claude did not forget Maître Frollo's words—"*If* there is a God,"—and many in Paris doubted this as well as the armorer.

Claude found his way to the school the next morning, and went up to where Jacques was standing near the fire as soon as he entered. "Where did you get to last night?" he asked.

"I think I might ask you that question," said Jacques, in an half-offended tone. "I went up and down the Rue Seine, calling you until I was tired."

"And I called you, and went stumbling about up one street and down another, until I found myself on the Petit Pont, and there I stayed for the night," said Claude.

"At the armorer's shop there—Frollo's?" said Jacques.

SEEMLY: *appropriate*
GAY: *light-hearted*

His companion stared. "Do you know him?" he asked, curiously.

"I have been there two or three times: he is very kind to all poor scholars; but my confessor has forbidden me to go again."

"Why?" asked Claude.

"Because he reads evil books, and loves not the Church. He is—"

But here the conversation was interrupted by Father Clement ordering the youths to go to their classes, and very soon the hum of lessons commenced. Books were scarce in those days, and Claude was compelled to look over a lad who sat next to him, for he had no money to buy books for himself. The youth was older than Claude, but with a gay, careless ease of manner that made him anything but a diligent scholar. In fact he was always in disgrace with his teachers for his remissness; but no one would ever have known it if they had not actually heard the reprimand given, for the merry face never showed anything but easy good humor, even when he was condemned to some punishment. One thing, punishment never made any difference to him—it was never allowed to interfere with his pleasure or comfort, for he always contrived to get out of it somehow. He would not hesitate to tell half-a-dozen falsehoods to excuse himself; and so he stood in very little awe of teachers or punishments either, and often set both at defiance.

This morning he did not feel disposed to give any attention to the task before him, and sat

REMISSNESS: *carelessness*
SET AT DEFIANCE: *defied*

playing with his iron pen, without attempting to use it. At length he turned his attention to Claude: "You are a stranger in Paris," he said.

"Yes, I come from Dauphiny," answered Claude, who rather liked the handsome, careless face of his schoolfellow.

"And you know nothing of Paris life?" said the other.

"I am a poor scholar," said Claude, glancing at his threadbare clothes.

His companion shrugged his shoulders. "You have no pleasure then—no fun in the streets when it gets dark," he said.

"I sang in the street last night," replied Claude.

"Bah! with that grim-faced Jacques, I suppose," he said, with a look of contempt.

"Rudolphe Mans, I must enjoin silence," said the teacher, a young monk.

"I am not talking," said Rudolphe, looking up with the most unblushing effrontery as he uttered this falsehood.

The young monk looked at him severely. "You are hindering your companion," he said, and passed on; for he knew it was of little use bandying words with Rudolphe.

"Why did you not contradict that," he said to Claude, as the monk passed out of hearing. Claude looked up in surprise. "How could I do so?" he said; "it was true enough, you know."

"Who cares for truth in these days?" said Rudolphe, with a contemptuous shrug. "Why, we should

ENJOIN: *order*
EFFRONTERY: *impudence*

not need to employ priests to perform masses for us, and there would be no candles or flowers on the altar of the Virgin and saints, if people were at the trouble of telling the truth always, and doing just what was right."

"Then you don't believe in religion," said Claude, quickly.

"Nay, nay, but I do. I am very religious," said Rudolphe, with an half-offended air; "everybody praises me for being so very devout; and I must be so, or life would not be so pleasant as it is."

Claude looked puzzled. "I do not understand," he said.

"Not understand," said Rudolphe; "why, 'tis easy enough. What do we pay our priests for but that they may say masses and get our sins pardoned. If we only keep a pretty good account of these, and go to confession regularly, and never cheat the Virgin of her candles or flowers, we may do almost as we like."

"And that is what you believe about religion?" said Claude, questioningly.

"What else should I believe?" said Rudolphe, with his usual gay indifference; "it's just what our priests teach us, and just the sort of religion to suit a Frenchman—no care, no trouble—the priests take all that for you, and you have only to believe what they tell you, and pay all that is due to the Church. I like that, and believe in the Church," he added, with a gay laugh.

"I don't," said Claude, frankly.

BANDYING WORDS: *arguing*

Rudolphe looked at him in amazement. "Why, the Church is perfect," he said.

"Then why don't the priests believe in it, and lead better lives," said Claude.

"I never trouble myself to think about such things as that," said Rudolphe; "it's enough for me if the holy father hears my confession and grants me absolution—he may amuse himself as he likes afterwards, so long as he does not interfere with my pleasure; and I know a good many people that think the same as I do."

This was perfectly true, and Rudolphe prided himself in being considered the most devout pupil in the school, and often made it stand him in good stead with his masters the monks. Today he was going to confession as he went home from school; and this being known he thought it was unnecessary to apply himself to his usual tasks, as he knew his masters would not keep him in beyond the appointed time to hinder him in this pious work, and so neither he nor Claude did much but gossip all the morning. At dinnertime both were reprimanded, and Rudolphe was allowed to leave, but with the understanding that he should stay in at the close of the afternoon school to perfect his neglected tasks. Claude was condemned to do this at once, and forbidden to speak to anyone until they were completed.

Rudolphe went off nodding saucily and knowingly at one or two who happened to be kept behind; and more than one grumbled at their

ABSOLUTION: *formal forgiveness of sins*

fortunate companion, who always managed to get off doing his tasks so easily. His look and nod had said, "I won't do them, you shall see!"

Claude seated himself at the further end of the room, and took up his book that he might not be disturbed; but a few minutes afterwards, when all the monks had retired, and there was no one to notice what was going on, Jacques came into the room.

He had been to buy something for dinner, for he knew Claude had no money, and he went up to him at once to show him his purchases. But as he drew near to the desk, Claude held up his finger to enjoin silence, and pointed to the book before him. Much as he wanted his dinner he would not take advantage of his master's absence to have it, or even talk to Jacques about it until his task was completed; and both waited until the master returned, and told Claude that he might leave his books and have his dinner.

Rudolphe, true to his resolution, contrived to leave in the afternoon without learning his lessons. Just before the school closed, a messenger came to say that Rudolphe was wanted at home immediately, as his mother had been taken ill. No one believed this tale but the masters, although Rudolphe pretended to be in great alarm when he heard it. Claude could not believe anyone would act so basely when he was told it was only one of Rudolphe's tricks: but when he went out with the rest, and saw him playing and capering a little way off, he could no longer doubt it.

SO BASELY: *in such a low manner*
CAPERING: *frolicking*

"How much will that trick cost you, my Rudolphe?" asked one, admiringly.

"A *petit blanc* for the messenger, and an extra candle for the shrine of St. Louis," said Rudolphe, with a burst of laughter.

"Ah, if I were but rich!" said his friend, with a sigh. "I get off all the lessons I can, but I cannot afford candles and—"

"Hush! I am going in here as well," said Rudolphe, as they reached the door of the church; and he tripped gaily in, dipped his finger in the consecrated water at the door, and bowed before the high altar, then passed to the shrine of the Virgin, where, kneeling down, he rattled over his beads in the most expeditious manner possible, and then returned to his less devout companions, who were standing near the door.

"That's all right," he said, as he joined them; "Now I can tell my confessor that I told a few lies, but repeated fifty *Aves* for them, and he will think it's about square, I know."

One or two seemed to think Rudolphe was not quite right in his notions of religion, but most of them agreed with him, because it was so convenient; and then so many of them could give proofs of their parents and friends acting upon the same principle, that the few like the poor scholar Jacques, who held that this was not what religion was intended to teach them, were cried down.

PETIT BLANC: *a small silver coin*
EXPEDITIOUS: *efficient*

Chapter III

The Monk of Clugny's Hymn

*T*HE two poor scholars were more fortunate in their search for the Rue St. Denis tonight, and Claude's heart beat high with the hope that he should soon see his noble friend Guillaume Farel. He did not intend to be seen by him, however; and he would not tell Jacques that he knew one of the students of the Sorbonne. But when they took their places under one of the overhanging stone gables of the corner house, he contrived to place himself in the shadow, where he could see everyone that passed, without being seen by them.

And here they commenced singing again their chants and hymns to the Virgin, for Jacques would never sing the ribald songs and satires on the priests and monks that were growing so much in fashion just now. It was as well, perhaps, for Claude that he would not, for the boy's spirit was already fierce and bitter enough without the knowledge of the cutting sarcasm of these, which everyone knew were too true. But he grew tired of "always singing the Latin chants," he said, after they had been

AVES: *the Catholic "Hail Mary" prayer*
RIBALD: *vulgar*

here about an hour. The truth was, he felt disappointed at not seeing young Farel; but Jacques did not understand this, and said, "I will teach you another hymn by and by."

"Another to the Virgin, I suppose," said Claude, with a sleepy yawn.

"No, it is not—there is not a word about the Virgin in it from beginning to end. It was written by a monk of Clugny. My uncle is in the same abbey in which he used to be; and he had a copy written out, which he sent to me before I left my home," replied Jacques.

Claude shrugged his shoulders. "I am weary of monkish hymns," he said.

"Nay, but this is different from all others you have ever seen," said Jacques, quickly. "Come now, I will read it to you, for I have the parchment securely in my bosom, and besides I have almost learned it by heart. We have a good store of *petit blancs* again," he added, touching the pouch at his girdle; "we can afford to have a rest now, and buy a torch as well."

It was quite impossible to thread the intricacies of the poorer streets without the aid of a torch, and so one was bought, lest they should lose their way and lose each other again; and then they set off in search of a lodging.

As soon as this was found, and their supper bought, Jacques drew out his parchment to read by the light of the flickering torch, which had been

put on the hearth to burn out, while Claude secretly made up his mind to go to sleep while Jacques
was reading.

But before the first verse was finished he was listening eagerly to the words of the monk's hymn.
They touched his heart as no words had ever
touched it before. Poor boy! he was feeling very
miserable. His conscience smote him for his neglect of religious duties; and whilst he was losing
all love for and faith in the rites of the Romish
Church, he yet felt a need of something better: he
knew not that God's Spirit was working upon him,
and the words of the hymn were as good seed falling into prepared ground.

> "The world is very evil,
>   The times are waxing late,
> Be sober and keep vigil,
>   The Judge is at the gate;
>
> The Judge that comes in mercy;
>   The Judge that comes with might,
> To terminate the evil,
>   To diadem the right."

Claude interrupted him at this point. "Read that
over again," he said eagerly; "I like those words—

> 'To terminate the evil,
>   To diadem the right.'"

he repeated.

Jacques began again, and read on for a few minutes; and then the delighted Claude again asked to

DIADEM: *crown*

have some lines repeated, and he slowly said them
after Jacques, that he might not forget them:

> "That peace—but who may claim it?
>   The guileless in their way.
>   Who keep the ranks of battle,
>   Who mean the thing they say.

But at length the interruptions from Claude became so frequent that Jacques declared he should
not be able to finish it before the torch went out.
There was no need now to urge him to learn some
of the verses to sing. Claude would have learned it
all at once if he could. This, however, was impossible; and so Jacques made some selections here and
there, for the poem was a very long one. The verses
they set themselves to learn that night Claude liked
better than all the rest, though Jacques declared
that the stanzas beginning "Jerusalem the Gold-
en," and "Brief Life is here our Portion,"[1] were the
sweetest, he gave way to his companion, and slowly
repeated:

> "Jerusalem exulting
>   On that securest shore,
>   I hope thee, wish thee, sing thee,
>   And love thee evermore.
>
> I ask not for my merit,
>   I seek not to deny
> My merit is destruction—
>   A child of wrath am I;

---

[1] Both are portions of the same hymn.

GUILELESS: *those who are honest and sincere*

But yet with faith I venture,
  And hope upon my way
For those perennial guerdons
  I'd labor night and day.

The best and dearest Father,
  Who made me and who saved,
Bore with me in defilement,
  And from defilement laved;

When in His strength I struggle,
  For very joy I leap,
When in my sin I totter,
  I weep, or try to weep;

And grace, sweet grace celestial,
  Shall all its love display,
And David's Royal Fountain
  Purge every sin away."

"And that was written by a monk three hundred years ago!" exclaimed Claude. "They are the very words I used to hear my father sing when I was only a child. I have never heard them since. He said they made him so happy, and that he hoped my mother and I and Margot would learn them someday, and go to David's Royal Fountain. I had quite forgotten all about it. I wish someone would tell us what they mean."

"We are only poor singing scholars," sighed Jacques; "and it was a holy monk who wrote this hymn."

"Yes, I can believe he was a holy man," said Claude; "and doubtless he would teach the poor people the things whereof he writes in this poem,

PERENNIAL: *continual, everlasting*
GUERDONS: *rewards*
LAVED: *washed*

and that would be quite different from the legends of the saints our monks teach in these days."

"Nay, nay; the monks teach what the Church commands," said Jacques, quickly. He would never hear a word against the holy fathers.

"Then the Church must have changed since the time of this Clugny monk," said Claude, boldly.

But Jacques shook his head. "You are over rash in your speech," he said. "As you know, our Church is perfect, and cannot err in her judgment in any matter."

"Yes—she is perfect; but 'tis in corruption," said Claude, hotly.

Jacques would not hear any more. "I think we had better go to bed," he said, quietly; and drawing from his bosom a little wooden image of the Virgin, he placed it on the wooden bench, and commenced his devotions at once.

Claude felt inclined to kneel down too, but he had little faith in the saints set forth by the monks now. Bernard of Clugny had set him wanting to know more of "David's Royal Fountain," that could "purge every sin away;" but how or where this knowledge was to be obtained he did not know; and so, instead of uttering the usual words, or drawing out his beads to tell over the accustomed *Aves*, he knelt down, and slowly repeated the words he had just learned, and then his thoughts went back to his mother again, and he said, half-aloud: "O God, bless my mother and Margot, if Thou hast no blessing for me."

TELL OVER: *repeat*

He would have gone to sleep happier that night than he had done for some time if it had not been for the disturbing thought that he ought not to think of these dear relatives now, and that perhaps his doing so would bring a curse upon their heads. For instead of growing up to be a good and holy man as they hoped, he was beginning to doubt what they believed, and to despise what they revered and loved. What would his mother think of him if she knew he had left off telling his beads, or going to mass? Besides which, he was sent to Paris that he might become a priest, and that he was sure he could never be now. So he felt himself to be cut off from his friends at home altogether.

Jacques could not understand how it was that Claude always wanted to go to the Rue St. Denis to sing of an evening, and was inclined to suspect that he wished to see someone who lived there. But night after night passed, and no one noticed either of them, beyond dropping a few coins in their hand, and so he could only think it was a whim of his companion's; while Claude waited and wondered how it was he never saw Guillaume Farel among the crowd of students that so often passed them.

It was but a scanty, uncertain living they could pick up singing in the streets of Paris; but the two boys made it suffice for their wants; and the spring was coming when they would be able to sleep under the shelter of some arch, or under a stall in the flower-market, and thus save the expense of a lodging. They had to do this now sometimes, for Jacques always went to the church of Nôtre Dame on every saint's day; and as Claude could not trust himself to sing alone in the streets, he usually paid a visit to his friend the armorer, where he was sure to hear all the gossip of the day.

Jacques frequently asked Claude to go with him to the church, telling him of the sweet chanting of the choristers, of the splendor of the services, and how nobly grand the old church looked, with its richly-stained glass windows and enshrined saints. But Claude only shrugged his shoulders and shook his head: he preferred hearing the armorer talk of the new books, and their satires on the clergy, which were so fast undermining men's faith in the Church they had hitherto looked upon as perfect. But one evening Jacques had begged so hard that he would go with him to Nôtre Dame that he could not refuse. So, instead of turning towards the Petit Pont as usual, he mingled with the stream of the people going towards Nôtre Dame.

The church was nearly full when they got there, and our two poor scholars were glad to get into a sheltered nook where they could see without being seen. The most devout portion of the congregation were not wasting their time by idly staring at their neighbors while waiting for the service to commence, but groups of them might be seen kneeling before the shrines of the various saints

CHORISTERS: *choir members*

choosing some special favorite to become their mediator. The image of the Virgin, in almost regal splendor, attracted the greatest number of worshipers; while the representation of her subject Son, by her side, was passed by almost unnoticed.

Jacques joined the crowd of devotees kneeling before the Virgin, and from watching him Claude looked at several others near. Among them was an insignificant, mean-looking old man, who seemed so absorbed in his devotions as to be quite unconscious of the crowd near. Close to him kneeled a noble-looking young man, who reminded Claude of his friend Guillaume Farel, and who seemed to pay the most obsequious attention to the old man when they rose from their knees and passed on to another shrine. Claude watched these two attentively: the simple, almost childish reverence with which they bowed before each saint attracted him strangely. "It is the Monseigneur Farel," he exclaimed at length, as the brilliant light from a silver lamp fell on the young man's face: "he is in Paris after all. But who can that mean, shabby-looking old man be?"

At this moment a tinkling of a small silver bell was heard. A door at the side opened, and a procession of priests advanced into the church; while the worshipers at the various shrines hastened back to their seats—all but the old man and Guillaume Farel, and they lingered until the last to finish their devotions.

MEAN: *unimportant*
OBSEQUIOUS: *devoted*

As might be expected, all the places near the altar were occupied, and they were glad to find room near our two poor scholars. Jacques had made good his retreat before, and as they paused just in front of them he whispered to Claude, "That is the learned professor, Dr. Lefèvre."

Claude opened his eyes in astonishment, although this explained Guillaume Farel's devoted attention to him. He had likewise heard his friend the armorer speak of the "little professor Lefèvre;" and yet he could hardly believe that the mean-looking man before him was the learned doctor that attracted so many to the Sorbonne.

Claude had come to look about him, rather than to worship; but he felt greatly rebuked by the devout attention paid to the service by his noble friend and the learned professor. In the chants and responses Dr. Lefèvre joined as heartily as the choristers themselves; and it was touching to see the childlike humility of this learned man, as he joined in the different parts of the service— Claude never forgot it. It puzzled him greatly now; and as he stood watching him he thought, "I wonder whether he has ever heard of 'David's Royal Fountain,' and could tell me what it is, and where I might find it. I would go on pilgrimage to seek that, for I cannot believe that these priests can 'purge every sin away;' they are themselves so guilty."

When they were in the street again, Jacques asked if he did not enjoy the service.

"It was all very splendid," said Claude; "but why can't we have the prayers in French, that everybody can understand, instead of Latin, that only a few can make out: it seems as though religion was only for the rich."

"What next will you find fault with?" said Jacques, in an half-offended tone.

It did not deter Claude from answering, however. "Why don't the friars preach about 'David's Royal Fountain,' and tell us what it is, instead of sending us to the priests? They cannot purge our sins away, I am sure, for they themselves are evil."

Claude could not see the look of horror in Jacques' face, but he noticed it in the tone of his voice, as he said, "Do you know that you are talking heresy?"

"Heresy; what is that?" asked Claude.

Jacques could not explain very fully. He only knew it was daring to disbelieve what the Church set forward as truth.

Claude shrugged his shoulders. "There are a good many heretics here in Paris then," he said; "for many doubt whether there is a God at all. I wish I knew," he added, with a sigh.

"I thought you said the other day you would not doubt this after reading the monk's hymn," said Jacques, quickly

"Well, I don't doubt it entirely; only I want to know something about Him, and the Church can tell us nothing but the legends of saints and the miracles of the Virgin."

"And are they not enough?" said Jacques.

"No! I want to hear something about 'David's Royal Fountain,' that this holy monk sings of. Jacques," he suddenly added, "we will sing our hymn outside the gates of the Sorbonne tomorrow; and if the little professor should give us some money, I will say, 'Dr. Lefèvre, can you tell us where "David's Royal Fountain" is? We are two poor scholars, and very ignorant; but would fain go on pilgrimage to this fountain to have our sins purged away.'"

Jacques smiled. "Dr. Lefèvre will tell you to go to your confessor with your sins," he said.

"But you will go and sing at the Sorbonne gate tomorrow?" persisted Claude.

"Yes, if you like; but we shall not get much money, you will see—the students are not rich like the citizens."

They had reached a sheltered nook where they had made up their minds to sleep tonight; after a scanty meal of rye bread, they crept in, and hid themselves before the guard should come round, for a mounted patrol went through the streets after nightfall, and closely questioned all loiterers.

WOULD FAIN: *desire to*

Chapter IV

At the Gate of the Sorbonne

CLAUDE thought more of going to the Sorbonne than he did of his lessons, while in school the next day, and, as a natural result, was detained for his inattention after the others left in the afternoon. For a wonder, Rudolphe Mans had failed to get off this punishment today, and so Claude was not alone in his captivity. He soon began to wish he was, for no sooner had the monks left, after locking the door and securing the grated windows to prevent their escape, than Rudolphe shut his own book with a bang that made the room reverberate, and then snatched Claude's away from him.

"We've had enough of books for today," he said, seating himself upon both the volumes. "We'll have some talk now. I want to tell you the latest news that has come to Paris. The new King of England, Henry VIII, has declared war against France, and is the head of the Italian league against us."

The news of a war between France and her old hereditary foes, the English, was pleasant enough to Claude; and in discussing the probability of the

REVERBERATE: *echo*
HEREDITARY: *inherited*

English archers and crossbowmen being seen in the streets of Paris, and drowned by hundreds in the Seine, he quite forgot his lessons for a time, until the approaching footsteps of the monk reminded them both of their neglected tasks.

Rudolphe gave Claude his book, and opened his own, clapping both hands to his head at the same time. "My head aches so much I cannot learn today," he said in a pitiable tone.

"I should like to know when you can learn," said Father Clement, sternly, taking the book from his hand, and dismissing him.

He then turned towards Claude: "Have you learned yours, or have you a headache too?"

Claude hung his head. "I have not learned it," he said.

"Why not?" asked the monk.

Claude still hung his head; but did not like to reply until the question was repeated, and then he said, slowly: "I have been talking."

This truthfulness was taken as defiance; and the monk applied the small whip he carried in his hand to Claude's back and shoulders, and then with a threat to write to Father Antoine by the next messenger going to Sainte Croix, and acquaint him with his behavior, he was pushed into the street, and almost knocked down Rudolphe, who was standing near.

Claude told him of the whipping he had received, but Rudolphe only shrugged his shoulders.

"It is your own fault," he said; "you should have said you were hungry. That would be true enough now, I should think," he added.

"Yes; but it did not prevent me learning," said Claude, trying to choke down his sobs.

"And you are going to be a priest, and can't or won't tell a lie," uttered Rudolphe. "Oh," he exclaimed the next minute, as he looked at Claude's serious face, "do you think anybody can be at the trouble of telling the truth always? We are alike, priests and people—we love pleasure, and hate care—and for the rest—well—" and he gave a most expressive shrug of the shoulders, and ran away as he saw Jacques approaching, for he always shunned him.

"Come, we shall be late before we reach the Sorbonne," said Jacques, without noticing the look of trouble on Claude's face.

"I don't care to go to the Sorbonne, or anywhere else," said Claude, dismally.

"Why, what is the matter?" asked Jacques, in a tone of surprise.

Claude told him of the whipping he had received, and that he had in some unaccountable way offended Father Clement, whom he had studiously endeavored to please. The matter was not such a mystery to Jacques, although he looked sorry when he heard of his companion's disgrace. Father Clement was his confessor, as well as his schoolmaster, and of course he had been obliged to divulge all that had passed between Claude and himself concerning the Church; but he had not intended bringing him into trouble through it. He wished he could avoid doing this again. But he must tell his confessor all that Claude said now, for he had been strictly enjoined to do so; and all private feelings of friendship must be sacrificed at the command of the Church.

Claude wondered what made his companion so silent, as they walked towards the Sorbonne. His own spirits had revived since he had had something to eat, for he was very hungry, although he could not truthfully say it had prevented him from learning. By the time the gates of the University were reached, he had almost forgotten his school troubles in the expectation of seeing the "little professor." Possibly, if he had been a grand-looking individual, Claude would not have summoned up courage enough to speak to him, for he shrunk back at the sight of some of the haughty-looking students; but he began the last verse of his favorite hymn, and pressed towards the front, as he saw Lefèvre approaching.

The learned doctor remembered the time when he came to Paris from Etaples, and was a "poor scholar" like these two. He paused a moment to listen, and put some money into Claude's hand. But it was not money the boy was looking for so anxiously, and he hardly noticed that it was offered, in his eagerness to speak. He placed himself directly

Claude Accosts Dr. Lefèvre

in the professor's way, and with a lowly reverence and trembling voice, said, "I have heard that you are a great and holy man, skilled in all kinds of learning: will you tell a poor scholar where 'David's Royal Fountain,' that 'purges sin away,' may be found?"

The professor looked at the lad, and then at the little knot of students standing round him, among whom was Guillaume Farel, although Claude had failed to notice him in his confusion.

One or two, who viewed religion in the same light as Rudolphe Mans, burst into a loud laugh, and exclaimed: "By St. Louis, the boy is mad."

The professor, however, checked their merriment at once, and looking kindly at Claude, said: "What is the matter with you, my poor lad?" He evidently thought him a little crazed.

"Why, it is Claude Leclerc, from Dauphiny," exclaimed Farel, edging himself to the front. "He is not mad," he said, turning respectfully towards Lefèvre. "What is it you would ask, Claude?" he said, addressing the boy.

But he was overwhelmed with confusion now, and could not utter a word; while whispered jokes passed round among the students about Claude and Farel being both mad.

"You were singing a hymn, I think," said Lefèvre, kindly; "suppose you come with me to my rooms and sing it again, and then I can hear your request. You will come with us," he said, addressing Farel.

CHECKED: *restrained*

The young man bowed, and the rest of the students began to disperse, when they found that no more fun was to be had, and the professor passed on, followed by Guillaume Farel and the two poor scholars.

"Why, where have you been hiding yourself, Claude?" asked young Farel; "I have expected to see you at some of the holy places I have been visiting lately in this city."

Claude hung his head and blushed. He could not bear to tell his friend that he had scarcely bowed to a single saint since he had been in Paris; but his native honesty overcame this at length, and he said: "I have not visited any of the holy relics."

Guillaume Farel looked surprised. "Then you have missed a great blessing," he said; "for many benefits are bestowed upon faithful souls that perform this service. Our noble professor of the Sorbonne is about to commence a very meritorious work, and write the lives and legends concerning the saints, as they are found in the calendar, for the help of pious souls, that they may not cease to offer their supplications to them."

There was not time to say more, for they had reached the professor's rooms. Claude and Jacques stood outside the door until invited to enter; and, when they looked round the room, they could not but be struck by the simplicity of all its appointments. There was no attempt at luxury. A black,

MERITORIOUS: *praiseworthy*
APPOINTMENTS: *furnishings*

oaken, high-backed chair, a table, and a few carved chests ranged against the wall, was all the furniture the room contained, except books, and a crucifix hung against the wall. But, beyond this, sheltered from the outer room by falling curtains of crimson silk-damask, and reached by two or three steps covered with rich carpet, was the professor's oratory. Although the evening had not yet closed in, it was ablaze with light from numerous wax candles set in silver sconces, which cast their rays on an exquisite figure of the Virgin, carved in alabaster, and surrounded with splendid vases of flowers. The gorgeous splendor of this alcove was in striking contrast with the rest of the apartments, and it could be seen that it was the professor's delight to adorn it with all that was most beautiful and costly.

After bowing towards this sacred spot, the old man seated himself in the high-backed chair, and motioned to the boys to commence their singing. Jacques would have changed the hymn for another, but Claude would not hear of it; and again they sung the monk of Clugny's verses, closing with the words—

> "And David's Royal Fountain,
> Purge every sin away."

"What is it you would ask me, my boy?" said the professor, as the two poor scholars paused. Claude advanced a step or two, and then kneeled down,

ORATORY: *private place of prayer*
SCONCES: *wall brackets*

for he began to fear that he had been overbold in his request now.

"I am but a poor scholar, and very ignorant," he said, in a trembling tone; "but I long to know where I may find 'David's Royal Fountain.' Is it in France, noble sir, that I could go on pilgrimage, and have my sins purged away in it?"

The professor looked at the eager, upturned face before him, and said slowly: "But have you forgotten the priests appointed by our Church to absolve sin?"

Claude cast his eyes upon the ground. "This hymn must have been written by a holy man, albeit he was a monk," he said; "and he says nought throughout of the priest purging our sins. Moreover, can a priest do this, when he himself is more unholy than other men?"

Jacques and Guillaume Farel looked aghast as they heard the bold words, and the professor seemed somewhat puzzled; but he did not lose his gentle, courteous bearing, for he saw that the boy was in earnest. Clever and learned as he was, however, he could not answer the question. He knew the philosophy of Plato, and could lecture on the ancient classic lore of Greece, but of "David's Royal Fountain," he knew nothing. He pondered for some minutes how he should answer this poor scholar, who had proposed a question more perplexing to him than any that had ever been asked by the most profound thinker in the University,

ABSOLVE: *grant pardon for*
AGHAST: *horrified*

and at length he said: "It is mystical language that is used, I doubt not, in this hymn; but I am about to enter afresh on the study of the lives of the saints, and if I discover aught that can teach me what the monk means by this language, I will not fail to let others know it too."

Claude could not but feel disappointed at this answer. He had hoped to have it made clear by the learned Dr. Lefèvre, and now it seemed that all he had gained by his adventure was to displease his best friend, Guillaume Farel; and he knew that Jacques would reproach him as well for daring to utter such bold words.

Farel was so greatly displeased that he would not notice Claude as he took his departure, although he acknowledged Jacques' lowly reverence with a quiet, grave bow, as became one of his noble descent.

This seemed to cut poor Claude to the heart. "It is very hard," he said as he reached the street; "I cannot believe that the Church is holy, as many suppose, and for this I am scorned and looked upon as worse than a thief."

"It is worse than robbery," said Jacques, in a severe tone; "and you—"

"I am not fit for a priest, I know; and I do not wish to become one," interrupted Claude.

"Hush! hush!" said Jacques, warningly. He really did not wish to hear these bold speeches, for he knew he must report them to his spiritual superior the next time he went to confession.

Chapter V

"David's Royal Fountain"

CLAUDE'S question seemed to awaken a train of thought in Dr. Lefèvre, that would not be put aside. After Guillaume Farel had left, and one of the heavy black-lettered books was placed on the table before him, he sat pondering over those two lines:

> "And David's Royal Fountain
> Purge every sin away."

He turned the pages of his book—an old chronicle of the wonders and miracles wrought by the saints. But it was very evident that he could not give all his attention to the subject in hand this evening; so at last he rose, and pushing aside his book, he took another from a chest close by him. "Our holy father the Pope has decreed that the writings of the Old and New Testaments shall henceforth be called the Holy Bible. I will search in that for the answer to the boy's question," he said, as he seated himself at the table once more.

It was not the first time Lefèvre had opened the Book, that, through his means was to commence the Reformation in France; but he had read it hitherto only as he would the works of Plato or Aristotle; but, now he came to it seeking for light and instruction that he had failed to find in his study of the lives of the saints. But light does not come all at once; Lefèvre did not obtain what he sought that evening. He turned to his projected work—"The Lives of the Saints," a portion of which was already published. To win the favor of these mediators he had constantly visited their shrines as his duties in the University would permit; but, instead of finding a growing satisfaction in this self-imposed task, the more he read the more disgust did he feel at the paltry, puerile nature of these fables, as compared with the sublimity of the Word of God.

Weeks and months passed away. At length, to everybody's surprise, he gave up his task, and devoted himself to the study of the Word of God alone. Bodæus, Cop, and Vatable were studying the Greek and Hebrew Scriptures, why should not he study them too? The satires that had been published on the lives of the clergy, he knew were but too true; but now he began to suspect that the Church he had hitherto regarded as holy, was in itself one huge lie. The doctrines of the Bible and the teaching of the Church, were utterly opposed to each other; and yet the Church professed to found its claims upon the authority of this Book.

PALTRY: *insignificant*
PUERILE: *trifling, silly*
SUBLIMITY: *exalted majesty*

No wonder it had been kept back, and the philosophy of men substituted for it; for, if it became known, men would no longer believe in the Roman Church.

The honest soul of the professor revolted from it more and more, as, by degrees, he became better acquainted with the sacred volume, and he determined to teach its life-giving truths to others. It did but need to be made known, he thought, and the minds of clergy and people would turn to it, and the Church would be purged of its errors and abuses. His heart glowed warmly with hope as he thought of this sometimes; and more than once he turned to Guillaume Farel, who was now his most favored pupil, and said, "My dear Guillaume, God will renew the world, and you will see it." Young Farel did not understand the old man's words then, but he often thought of them afterwards.

The fables of the Romish Breviary no longer satisfied the mind of Lefèvre; and he turned from them to the study of St. Paul's Epistles, and learned to understand the monk of Clugny's lines about "David's Royal Fountain." He learned to see that "the blood of Jesus Christ cleanseth us from all sin,"[1] and that the power to do this has never been granted to any man or any class of men—that it is God's free gift to sinners; and that, believing this, they are justified and will be made holy by the Spirit of God.

In a few months he began to teach these truths to the assembled students in the halls of the Sor-

[1] I JOHN 1:7
BREVIARY: *the Roman Catholic book of prayers*

bonne, and the strangeness and novelty of such teaching drew many others to listen to the "little professor." His voice was the first in France to proclaim the battle-cry of the Reformation—justification by faith. "It is God alone, who, by His grace, through faith, justifies unto everlasting life," he said.

He often looked for the poor scholar who had asked him where he might find "David's Royal Fountain," as he passed out of the Sorbonne gates; but he never saw him now. Guillaume Farel, too, remarked that he had not seen Claude for some months—not since he went home to see his parents at the end of the year. Claude had told him then that Father Clement was greatly displeased with him because he had neglected to go to confession, and had sent various complaints to Father Antoine at Sainte Croix, though what the complaints were he did not know.

Farel was not surprised to hear this. He was rather glad than otherwise; for he thought the lad must have formed some very bad companionships since he had been in Paris, or he would never have neglected the worship of the saints and relics, and spoken as he had done to Dr. Lefèvre. Now, however, that months had passed, and he was not to be seen, he began to grow anxious; and at length determined to call at the school, and inquire of the monks what had become of their pupil.

It happened, however, that Farel's intimacy with the "little professor," who was preaching such strange doctrines at the Sorbonne, had reached the ears of Father Clement, who had already begun to smell heresy in the declaration that man can be justified by the grace of God alone; and so, when he heard from Jacques who his visitor was, he declined to answer any of his questions about Claude. Jacques himself did not know anything but that his companion had been detained in the schoolroom one afternoon, and had not been seen or heard of since.

Guillaume Farel was somewhat alarmed at this. There had always been some mystery about his being sent to Paris at all, and he began to grow more uneasy. He had heard strange tales told here in Paris, of people being put out of the way by the monks, which he could not wholly disbelieve; and he began to fear that his honest-hearted young friend had been one of these.

He was not particularly anxious that Claude should meet the professor of the Sorbonne just now; for the fact was, he thought these new and strange doctrines, striking as they did at the root of all the worship and reverence the Church had decreed should be paid to the saints, were highly dangerous. He himself had commenced the study of the sacred Scriptures; but he had been afraid to believe what the Word of God declared was the truth, because it differed so greatly from the teaching of the Church.

"I do not understand these things. I must give

a very different meaning to the Scriptures, from that which they seem to have. I must keep to the interpretation of the Church," he had said to one of his companions; and shortly after he gave up the study entirely, for one of the doctors of Sorbonne reproved him very sharply for doing it. "No man ought to read the holy Scriptures before he has learned philosophy, and taken his degree in arts," exclaimed the doctor. It was not often he had to reprove a student for giving his attention to sacred subjects; for half the young men in the University were giving all their attention to the acting of dramas and plays, as though they were to be mountebanks for the rest of their lives.

There was little fear of Guillaume Farel wasting his time in this way. After giving up the study of the Scriptures, he devoted himself more earnestly than ever to the worship of the saints; and his reason for seeking Claude just now was that he might accompany him to the cells of some holy hermits, living in a wood just outside Paris. Young Farel had visited them several times before, and shared in their fasts and long vigils, and other austerities; and he hoped that their influence and example would win Claude back to his reverence and love for the Church. Now anxiety for the lad's fate was added to this wish, and he determined to make inquiries for him before visiting the hermits.

MOUNTEBANKS: *sellers of quack medicines who attracted customers by telling stories*
CELLS: *huts or caves*

Waylaying the scholars, he spoke to Rudolphe Mans, and asked if he knew anything of Claude. For a moment Rudolphe was alarmed. "He has left Paris, has he not?"

"I do not know; I ask you," replied Farel.

"And I have asked Frollo, the armorer," said Rudolphe.

"Who is Frollo, the armorer?" asked Farel.

"Any poor scholar can tell you, I wot, for he is a friend to them," answered Rudolphe, wondering what a young noble like Guillaume Farel could have to say to a poor singing-boy.

"Where does this Frollo live?" inquired Farel.

If he had had anything to do with the gayer portion of the students he need not have asked this question; for the armorer not only sold but lent armor and weapons of all sorts, and some of his best customers were among the students of the Sorbonne.

Rudolphe opened his eyes, and there was a touch of contempt in his tone as he said: "You do not know Frollo, of the Petit Pont?"

Farel did not stay to reply to this. He had gained the intelligence he wanted, and hurried away at once towards the place named.

But by the time he reached the armorer's shop, Frollo had finished his supper, and gone out for his usual evening gossip. He found it was highly advantageous to be able to supply his customers, the students, with any little bit of scandal, or the report

WOT: *know*

of anything going on at court, or among the fashionable circles of Paris. There were no newspapers in those days; and so people were dependent, in a great measure, on these gossip-loving people for all they knew of what was going on around them.

Madame looked vexed when she came into the shop, and saw a student there. She darted back for a moment to say to Babette that she must not come out, for she did not choose that the girl should be looked at by one of the gallants of the Sorbonne. She remarked, however, that Guillaume looked very grave for a comedy-loving student, and paid very little heed to the weapons hanging round the shop.

"I wish to see the armorer," he said, as he saw Madame.

"My husband is not at home, Monsieur; but I can show you anything you may wish to see," answered Madame.

Farel shook his head. "I do not wear armor," he said, with a smile.

"But for the dramas or comedies we have all kinds of braveries," said Madame; "doublets of velvet, as well as coats of mails."

But the young man again shook his head. "I did but want to ask your husband a question," he said; "I am anxious to gain tidings of a poor scholar who was in the school of St. Germain l'Auxerrois, Claude Leclerc."

BRAVERIES: *showy clothing or accessories*
DOUBLETS: *tight-fitting jackets*

"We often have poor scholars here," said Madame; "my husband holds it a duty to help such. But I do not know this Claude Leclerc by name: it often happens that we do not hear their names at all," she added.

"He is from Dauphiny," said Farel; "he came here about eighteen months ago, but has not been seen lately."

While he was speaking, Frollo himself came hurrying in for something he had forgotten. He looked from the student to his wife, wondering that the counter was not spread with goods.

"Monsieur has come to ask about a poor scholar from Dauphiny," said Madame.

"Claude Leclerc?" said Frollo, quickly.

"Yes, can you tell me aught concerning him?" said Farel.

"Nay, nay, cannot you? I have sought him everywhere," said the armorer; "for I had a special liking for the lad."

"If he had left Paris, would he have let you know his intention, do you think?" asked Farel.

"Yes, I am sure he would, if he had been able," said the armorer. "But I do not think he has left," he added, in a mysterious tone.

The young noble looked at him curiously. "What do you mean?" he asked.

Frollo shrugged his shoulders. "The Seine tells not its secrets," he said, in a whisper.

Guillaume Farel stared. "Do you think the lad is drowned?" he exclaimed.

"I didn't say so, Monsieur," answered Frollo, beginning to see that he had spoken incautiously to this stranger. "It might be so, you know," he added; "the nights are dark, and he might have gone to where the women wash their clothes, and have fallen in."

Farel looked at the speaker steadily. "You do not think this is likely, though," he said. "You have some other reason for saying this. Do not be afraid to speak to me. I am his friend, and a friend, too, of the noble professor, Dr. Lefèvre."

At the name of Dr. Lefèvre, Frollo's face changed, the look of caution passed away, and he said, "Then I may tell you freely of my doubts."

Madame, however, reminded her husband that customers might come in, and overhear more than was wished; and so Frollo invited the young student to walk into the room at the back of the shop, where Babette sat busy with her distaff. Madame thought she had better go with them, that she might sit before Babette, and screen her from observation; and likewise warn her husband, by an occasional look, if he got talking upon dangerous topics.

As soon as they were seated, Guillaume Farel said: "You think Claude has been unfairly dealt with, then, Frollo?"

The armorer bowed his head. "I know somewhat of his history," he said; "and that these priests and monks have no favor towards him."

"And you think these brothers of St. Germain l'Auxerrois have got rid of him?" said Farel.

"I do!" answered the armorer; "it would not be the first time that such things have been done here in Paris, and it will not be the last if the Church continues in power."

Young Farel opened his eyes. "*If* the Church continues in power," he repeated. "Do you think she is likely to lose that power then?" he asked.

"Pardon, Monsieur, I am overbold perhaps in offering my opinion, which cannot be worth much, seeing it is only that of a poor armorer; but I hear that our learned professor of the Sorbonne teacheth such strange new doctrines now, that the whole world will be turned upside down if men will but embrace them."

"But they will not embrace them," said Farel, quickly; "for they are founded upon the Scriptures, and not the teaching of the Church."

"Pardon, Monsieur; but is not this same Book— the Scriptures—the Word of God, and commanded by our Lord Pope to be called the Holy Bible? And is it not upon this that all the laws of the Church, as well as her doctrines and claims, are said to be founded?"

Farel looked confused, and knew not how to reply. He had forgotten that the Church pretended to have this Word of God as her authority.

Frollo feared he had offended his visitor.

"I trust Monsieur will pardon my boldness of speech," he said; "I am only an ignorant and unlearned man, and can never hope to see this

Word of God. But I should greatly like to do so, and to hear what our professor of the Sorbonne teacheth."

"Well, that you shall do, if you wish," said Farel, quickly, anxious to assure him that he was not offended, and feeling grateful for the kindness he had shown to poor Claude; "I can take you to hear one of Dr. Lefèvre's lectures next week, if you will not mind standing in a crowd."

"Mind standing in a crowd!" exclaimed Frollo, forgetting everything else in his delight. "I would do anything to hear him."

So an arrangement was made at once, and Farel took his departure, feeling still more anxious about Claude.

Chapter VI

Strange News for Paris

FROLLO was at the place appointed by Farel, near the Sorbonne, the following week, as anxious to hear the learned professor as any of the students in the University. Both had made inquiries, too, in the interim, hoping to gain some tidings of Claude; but a silence as impenetrable as that of the grave seemed to have closed round him. The monks of St. Germain l'Auxerrois would tell nothing, and no one else had the power, and so the gloomiest forebodings filled the minds of his two friends.

There was not a little joking among the students when the dress of Frollo was seen among the crowd pressing into the hall where Dr. Lefèvre was to lecture; but by degrees these grew less noisy, and by the time the insignificant figure of the little professor appeared, all else was forgotten, and everyone was waiting with eager gravity for the sonorous voice to ring out in its clear tones the wonderful news of God's love to men. Every-

GRAVITY: *earnestness*
SONOROUS: *rich, impressive*

one was eagerly anxious to hear today's lecture, for
the doctor had promised to show the agreement
in the apparent opposition of the teaching of St.
James and St. Paul on the subject of justification
by faith.

This lecture was delivered in French instead of
Latin, as many were; and so Frollo could understand every word that was said, although he had
scarcely more than heard of the two apostles, St.
Paul and St. James, until today. Dr. Lefèvre stated,
in clear and concise language, St. Paul's declaration: "Being justified freely by His grace through
the redemption that is in Christ Jesus: whom God
hath set forth to be a propitiation through faith in
His blood, to declare His righteousness for the remission of sins that are past, through the forbear-
ance of God; to declare, I say, at this time His righteousness: that He might be just, and the justifier
of him which believeth in Jesus."[1]

After speaking of the freeness and fullness of
the redemption that had been wrought by the
death of Christ, and that this was offered to all,
and might be accepted by all without the purchase
of good works, he turned to the apostle St. James,
and read, "Every good gift and every perfect gift is
from above, and cometh down from the Father of
lights."[2] "Now," said Lefèvre, "who will deny that
justification is the good and perfect gift?"

But some objected that St. James said, "Faith
without works is dead."[3]

---

[1] ROMANS 3:24-26   [2] JAMES 1:17   [3] JAMES 2:20
PROPITIATION: *way of gaining favor with God*
REMISSION: *forgiveness*

"True," answered the professor. "But if we see a man moving, the respiration that we perceive is to us a sign of life. Thus works are necessary, but only as signs of a living faith which is accompanied by justification. Do eyesalves and lotions give light to the eye? No, it is the influence of the sun. Well, then, these lotions and these eyesalves are our works. The ray that the sun darts from above is justification itself."[1]

Farel and his companion listened earnestly and attentively to this teaching, and the young student, as well as the armorer, was deeply impressed. The one had been laboring incessantly of late to establish a righteousness of his own, and the other had loudly declared there was no such thing as righteousness in heaven or earth; and now both their hearts were touched—different as was their condition in every particular—by this wonderful truth, that it is God's free gift to man, given out of His abounding love to man, and wrought by the death of Christ.

Frollo went home, not to boast of the distinction conferred upon him, in being admitted to the professor's lecture, but to think and talk over with his wife the wonderful news he had heard. It would be as new and strange to her, he knew, although she was so regular and devout in her attendance at Church and confession, and she and Babette were constantly doing something for the shrine of the Virgin, in their own little oratory upstairs.

[1] D'Aubigné's *History of the Reformation*

While these things were thus being discussed, and Madame was looking carefully through her calendar of saints to make sure that St. Paul and St. James were among them, Guillaume Farel, in the quiet of his own room, was once more studying the writings of these apostles, to see if these things affirmed by Dr. Lefèvre were so in very truth. Then again arose the question, why had the Church concealed this doctrine for so many ages? Then came another question, dare he believe the evidence of the plain ungarbled Word of God before the interpretation the Church chose to put upon that Word? Had he the right of private judgment in matters of conscience, instead of following the judgment of the Church and his spiritual directors? It was not easy to answer these questions. It cost him excessive grief and pain to cast aside all the reverence, and faith, and trust, he had ever reposed in the teachings of the Church.

But he was not left alone in this struggle. He did not shrink from the pain it cost him, and the Spirit of God upheld him through all, and brought him into the clear light of the gospel at last. Now he could listen with joy and satisfaction to the evangelical truths taught by the learned professor Lefèvre; and so earnest was he to communicate the benefits he received from the doctor's teaching, that he frequently went to the armorer's shop on the Petit Pont to help Frollo in his seeking.

UNGARBLED: *undistorted*
REPOSED: *placed*
EVANGELICAL TRUTHS: *truths based on the Scriptures*

It was not so easy for the armorer to obtain knowledge and guidance in his longing after divine truth, for where could he go for instruction. The Bible was a sealed book to him. The Romish Breviary gave the fabled doings of saints and martyrs, which he had long since given up as unworthy the attention of a sensible man. No one preached or taught the things spoken of by Dr. Lefèvre, anywhere in Paris, and the gates of the Sorbonne were only open to the rich and learned.

Babette was struggling up to the light in a simple fashion of her own. A little oratory had been prepared for her, in an alcove of her own bedroom; for, as an only child she was greatly indulged; and her mother began to look upon her as a woman, although she treated her to a sharp box of the ears occasionally.

With her oratory, however, she did not interfere, and Babette kept her own secret about the changes she had effected there. A short time after her father's visit to the Sorbonne, and after hearing him speak again and again of the death of Christ as being the means of man's salvation, she thought it was hardly fair that the Virgin Mary should monopolize all her worship; and so one day, with trembling hands and many misgivings, she quietly took down the image of the Virgin from its throne, and placed a little crucifix she had bought in its stead.

All day she felt anxious and terrified when she thought of what she had done; and she was half-afraid when she went upstairs to draw the curtain and peep in, lest she should see the crucifix thrown down and the dethroned figure mounted in its place. She half-expected that some such terrible miracle as this was going on upstairs in her little oratory when she saw her confessor walk into the shop to make some purchase, and inquire why she had not been to confession lately. Her mother did not know she had neglected this duty, but she would know it now; and doubtless Father Pierre would tell her that an angel had visited him in his monastery to complain of the trouble he had been put to in coming to replace the image of the Virgin again. Such miracles had been known to take place again and again in the churches and monasteries in Paris, and why should it not in her oratory?

Father Pierre left, however, without saying a word about this, and Madame had succeeded in convincing him that it must have been one of his other penitents that had absented herself instead of Babette. She felt more sure of her daughter in this particular than she did of the priest, for he was one who loved a tankard of wine too well ever to care much about anything else, and she doubted not he had been drinking and forgotten all the girl had told him.

Much relieved that Father Pierre left without mentioning her oratory, Babette ran upstairs in some trepidation to see whether any change had been effected in its arrangement, and was much

PENITENTS: *people who confess their sins to a priest*
TREPIDATION: *anxiety*

relieved to find her crucifix just where she had left
it. She could not all at once leave off her prayers
to the Virgin; but from this time the Lord Jesus,
instead of His mother, became her chief object of
worship. She had but an imperfect idea of what He
had done for her; but her heart went out in love towards Him such as she had never felt towards the
saints, and thus dimly and darkly was she struggling onward towards the light which many earnest souls hoped would spread from the Sorbonne
to all France.

It was a disputed point with Frollo and his wife
whether the newly-invented art of printing would
do good or harm in the world. Madame contended
that men had lived and the Church had prospered
hitherto without books being multiplied beyond
what the monks could supply by copying, and that
the attempt to do anything beyond this must come
from the evil one, and would tend to draw men
away from the Church. But a few months after
this—early in the year 1512—she was constrained
to alter this opinion. Guillaume Farel came to tell
them the news that the printing-presses were to be
set to work on the "Commentary on St. Paul's Epistles," written by Dr. Lefèvre. Much more eagerly
than his "Lives of the Saints" would his new work
be read, and hundreds would hail it with delight
who could not hear his living voice.

Madame had always heard the "little professor"
spoken of as a most learned and devout Catholic,

CONSTRAINED: *obliged*

and she was glad to hear that the new invention was to be used for other purposes besides publishing satires on the priests and monks. She did not believe the scandal which some few had begun to circulate, that the doctrine he taught was only to lead men to live unholy lives, without fear of the consequences. Frollo told Farel of this charge against Lefèvre.

"Well, I can give you an opportunity of being able to disprove that," said the young man; "if you will come to the Sorbonne tomorrow, I can secure your admission to hear another lecture from Dr. Lefèvre. Will it suit you to come?" he asked.

Suit him? The armorer was willing to sacrifice any pleasure or gain to secure such an opportunity. The Word of the Lord was indeed precious in those days. He was at the Sorbonne gates long before the hour named, so fearful was he of losing the chance of hearing this lecture; but he need not have feared—Guillaume Farel was not one to forget a promise.

They were indeed strangely precious words that rang through the arched roof of the Sorbonne hall that day—words that were spirit and life to more than one who heard them, although they were the heralds of another fierce conflict in his soul. Guillaume Farel had still clung with some fondness to the worship of the saints as well as Christ. He could not let go this the last hold of Romanism, and trust to Jesus only as the one Mediator as well as the

PRECIOUS: *scarce*
HERALDS: *signs*

all-sufficient Savior; but this lecture was destined
to strike away this last prop.

"Religion," said the professor, "has but one
foundation, one object, one head—Jesus Christ,
blessed forevermore! Alone hath He trodden the
winepress. Let us not, then, call ourselves after St.
Paul or Apollos or St. Peter, for the cross of Christ
alone openeth the gates of heaven, and shutteth
the gates of hell. Oh, ineffable exchange! the in-
nocent One is condemned, and the criminal acquitted. The Blessed One is cursed, and he who
was cursed is blessed. The Life dies, and the dead
live. The glory is covered with shame, and he who
was put to shame is covered with glory."[1]

But the lecture was not wholly taken up with
doctrines alone. Many had said that if justification
by faith were believed, instead of the efficacy of
good works, men would live solely after their own
pleasure. But if any had come there hoping to be
able to reconcile themselves to believing the new
doctrines and still following their evil lives, they
were greatly disappointed.

"If thou art a member of Christ's Church thou
art also a member of His body," said Lefèvre; "and
if thou art a member of Christ's body, thou art full
of the Divinity—'for in Him dwelleth the fullness
of the Godhead bodily.'[2] Oh, if men could but
understand this privilege, how purely and holily
would they live; and they would look upon all the
glory of this world as disgrace in comparison with

[1] D'Aubigné's *History of the Reformation*
[2] COLOSSIANS 2:9
INEFFABLE: *impossible to express in words*

that inner glory which is hidden from the eyes of the flesh."

To Farel the first part of this lecture was the most startling. That God in Christ should be the sole object of men's worship, was something he could not grasp at once. Christ *and* the saints of the Romish calendar he had accepted; but Christ *alone*—his soul stood aghast at the thought of giving up all the divinities he had hitherto worshiped; and there ensued another struggle, as fierce as that over the authority of Scripture and the right of private judgment. But the victory was not a doubtful one, although the battle had been long and severe. The young student yielded himself to the guidance of the Spirit of God; and after diligent study of God's Holy Word—for upon a question so momentous as this he would accept the judgment of no man, not even such a revered teacher as Dr. Lefèvre—he would accept the Word of God alone as his guide in such matters, and that expressly stated: "There is one God and one mediator between God and men, the man Christ Jesus."[1]

Lessons scarcely less powerful or convincing did the armorer carry home with him to the Petit Pont. He had said, in his pride and arrogance, there was no God—men were left to manage their own affairs as they could; but now he heard that salvation, full, free, and perfect, had been wrought for men by the Son of God, and was offered for their acceptance. Why the Church had concealed this

[1] I Timothy 2:5

EFFICACY: *effectiveness*

free gift so long he could not tell; but he doubted not that now the great truth had been rescued from the darkness, many like Farel would be found willing to spread the knowledge of it, and the Church would enter upon a new and bright era.

He could not help wondering whether this light had touched other minds in Europe as well as Dr. Lefèvre's. It was a question the armorer could scarcely hope to have answered, for it was one that sometimes crossed the professor's own mind; and he scarcely dared to hope that it was so, for if it had been, the Sorbonne, as the first University in Europe, must have heard of it.

But God was working in other hearts, nevertheless, although as yet nothing was heard. Just at this time a humble monk was on his way from Germany to Rome, on some business connected with his order, and the question that above all others occupied his mind was this very question of justification by faith. In his lonely vigils in the monastery at Erfurth, the Spirit of God had revealed this truth to his soul, but he could not fully grasp it yet; but ere he retraced his homeward steps it would burst upon his mind like the sun breaking through the darkness, and then Luther would proclaim it to all the world.

Another earnest-hearted, zealous friend of the papacy was at this time on his way across the Alps from Switzerland, to aid the holy father in upholding his spiritual power, by the help of the confederate swords of his followers. But the student Farel and the soldier Zwingle would rejoice together over other conquests than those he now hoped to make; and Geneva would testify that the Spirit of God spoke with no uncertain voice to the learned and noble student, or the bold and fearless soldier. But to France was given the honor of being the first where this mighty voice was heard and translated. She might have been the pioneer of the glorious reformation in Europe; but she counted the honor of little worth, and scorned the voice that bid her arise and shine, and to this day she is paying the penalty of her scorn.

Chapter VII

An Unexpected Meeting

"VIVE le Roi! Vive le Roi!" shouted the people of Paris, as they pressed forward on to the Petit Pont to greet their king, Louis XII, on his return from the castle of Blois. It was a cold day in February; but what cared the people for that, when their good king Louis was about to visit his capital.

The king rode on horseback; and by his side, in a dress more rich and showy, rode his nephew, Francis of Valois, a tall, handsome youth, who smiled and bowed, especially if he saw a pretty face in the crowd. After the richly-caparisoned horses came the queen's litter, in which rode the little princess Renée, with her mother; and then the beautiful duchess of Angoulême, the sister of Francis, on a white palfrey; then the velvet-curtained litter of the duchess of Savoy, the mother of Francis and Marguerite, who spent most of her time at court, eagerly watching the chances of her son to succeed his uncle, for it had been predicted that he would be the next king.

VIVE LE ROI!: *Long live the King!*
RICHLY-CAPARISONED: *richly-decorated*
PALFREY: *a saddle horse other than a war horse*

To make sure of this, she had contrived to have him betrothed already to the king's eldest daughter, Claude, lest the Salic law, prevailing in France, should be reversed in her favor, and she should be allowed to succeed her father, for Louis, to his great grief, had no son.[1]

Today he was looking very anxious; and well he might, for news had just come that his old foes, the English, were about to embark with a hundred thousand men, and invade the southern portion of his kingdom. He had likewise another cause of anxiety, more remote, perhaps, in its consequences, but not less sure. A book had been written by Cardinal Cajetan, to prove that the pope was the absolute monarch of the Church; and this he was about to lay before the learned doctors of the Sorbonne, and ask their opinion upon it.

The king knew that he was no favorite with the Pope; for some years before, when urged by his Holiness to enter upon a war against the Waldenses, he had refused to do so. Instead of responding to the pope's cry, "To arms, and trample these heretics under foot, as venomous serpents," Louis had asked what their crime had been, and sent his confessor to gather testimony as to their character and conduct. When he heard of their piety, industry and peacefulness, he swore by all the saints in the calendar that they were better Christians than himself, and should not be interfered with. King in his own dominions Louis naturally wished to

[1] Freer's *Life of Marguerite of Valois*
PIETY: *devotion to God*
INDUSTRY: *diligence in business*

be; but he would not, if what the cardinal had advanced in his book was true; for if the pope was absolute monarch of the Church, he would have the right to incite his subjects to rebellion, absolve them from all national allegiance, and leave the sovereign but a king in name.

Scarcely less anxious than the king himself were some of the doctors of the Sorbonne to ascertain what was the rightful position of the pope; and all Paris was in agitation while this matter was pending. Frollo, standing at the door of his shop, watching the king's train of courtiers and household servants, could talk of nothing else; while Madame and Babette, from an upper window, discussed the dresses of the ladies, and indulged in surmises as to whether the young duchess Marguerite had learned to love her husband any better yet, for report said that she loved her brother Francis far more than the Count d'Angouleme, while he paid more court to his sister than to his betrothed.

The subject of the cardinal's book, and the invasion of France by the English, was enough to occupy the citizens' minds for the present, and turned men's minds more than ever in the direction of the Sorbonne. How the matter would be decided no one could tell at first. At length it was announced that James Allmain, one of the youngest doctors, but a man of profound genius and indefatigable application, had prepared a refutation, to be read before the faculty of theology.[1] They received it with

---

[1] Dupin's *Ecclesiastical History*

INDEFATIGABLE: *tireless*

the greatest applause, and thus the whole University seemed impatient to throw off the papal yoke.

No wonder that Lefèvre's young disciples everywhere preached the doctrine of liberty, and claimed it for themselves; or that many joined their ranks merely from the love of learning, or disgust at the superstitions of the Church, who yet failed to see that liberty did not mean license to commit sin.

From the noise and confusion of the great city, Guillaume Farel was at length compelled to retire; and in the early summer he resolved to pay a visit to his home. Again did he renew his inquiries about Claude, for he did not like to return to Dauphiny without being able to bear tidings of him; but all in vain—no one had seen him now for nearly two years; and Farel could only adopt the armorer's belief, that he had died, by fair means or foul.

Another February came round, and the people of Paris had again turned out in the cold to meet their king. But there were no shoutings or songs of welcome this time. A deep gloom, deeper than that of the sullen cloudy day seemed to hang over the whole city. Men only spoke to each other in subdued tones. The women who were abroad wore dresses of black cloth. The houses and balconies were draped with black; for this was no holiday festival, and their king was overwhelmed with grief. His dearly-beloved wife, Anne of Bretagne, was to be buried today at St. Denis; and his loyal subjects

would show their sympathy with his sorrow by closing their shops, and leaving their usual employ-
ments to line the streets leading from Nôtre Dame
to the place of sepulture.

By and by the faint sound of chanting was heard;
and in a minute or two the low wailing notes of the
Miserere could be distinguished. Then the crowd
swayed backwards and forwards, and pressed each
other more closely in their eagerness to struggle
to the front, and obtain a view of the long train
of ecclesiastics that would precede the funeral. A
huge silver cross was the first thing seen, borne
before one of the Church's highest dignitaries. He
was dressed in richest robes of purple and crimson damask, his train borne by six little boys in
white surplices. Then came a train of priests, in
white surplices, and monks in the dresses of their
various orders, chanting the *Miserere* and office for
the dead. Scarce a heart in all that crowd but was
touched with sorrow for the death of their queen,
for she was greatly beloved by her subjects.

The students and doctors of the Sorbonne, who
were not taking part in the spectacle, had come
out to see it; and among these was Guillaume
Farel. But before the first notes of the singing were
heard, his attention had been attracted by a poor
woman and two girls on the opposite side of the
narrow street. They had taken up their position
at the front of the crowd; and, protected by the
projecting gable of a house, all the elbowing and

SEPULTURE: *burial*
SURPLICES: *long tunics with sleeves*
OFFICE: *ceremony*

pushing failed to displace them. They were not Parisians he could tell by the frightened looks of the two girls, and the imploring glances they now and then cast towards their mother. But she saw nothing of this. Her eager gaze was fixed upon the point where the procession would first appear, and her hands were clenched in the intense excitement of her eagerness. Now and then she unclosed them to make the sign of the cross on her breast or forehead, and her lips moved as though she were rapidly repeating the Rosary of the Virgin; but her eyes never wandered from the distant corner of the street. She wore the dress of a Seine washerwoman; and the elder girl did the same—but that of the younger was more like that of a Dauphinese peasant. It was this that attracted his attention first to the group; and the more he looked, the more convinced he became that it was the widow Leclerc, with her two children, Marguerite and Fanchon.

He did not know that they were in Paris. He had not visited home since the previous summer; neither had he heard, by letter or message, what was going on in the village. Those were not the days of railroads and post offices. If people wished to communicate with their friends at a distance, they must send a special messenger; or wait until some traveler called that way, to whom they could entrust a packet.

But although Farel had not heard that the Leclercs had come to Paris, he was convinced they were before him now; and he would have crossed the road, and spoken at once, but that a party of arquebusiers were patrolling up and down to keep the narrow roadway clear. So he could only stand and watch; and become more and more convinced that it was the widow from his native village, and that she was now eagerly looking and expecting to see her son among the crowd of priests.

He could only look at her in tenderest pity and compassion, when the silver cross appeared; and then the procession began slowly to defile past, and the group was completely hidden from view. They were almost forgotten in the interest of watching the spectacle, and listening to the mournful, wailing chant, and thinking of the virtues of the departed queen; when all at once, rising above the sound of the singing and regular tramp of bare and sandaled feet, rose the piercing shriek of a woman. There was, at the same moment, a temporary stoppage in the procession; and one or two of the superiors, pushing aside their cowls, looked back to see the cause of the interruption. But it was only momentary. The cold, hard faces of these men showed no emotion: they were dead to the world and all the ties of relationship in it; and they went on with their monotonous chant, and no one would have known that anything had happened, but that some remarked that a monk must have dropped from his place, as there were only two abreast in one line, where there should have been three.

ARQUEBUSIERS: *soldiers carrying arquebuses, or guns*
DEFILE: *march by in a line*
HOST: *bread used in communion*

"What is it? what has happened?" asked young Farel of an acquaintance standing near.

The other shook his head. He had no time to answer, for the Host carried high above everybody's head, and surmounted by a rich canopy of cloth of gold, had just come into view; and the whole multitude went down upon their knees, and with bowed heads waited until it had passed.

When they rose again, Farel repeated his question. "Well, 'tis whispered that a monk dropped dead at the sight of yonder image of the Virgin. 'Tis more likely to be a case of poisoning among the holy brothers; but they will have a fine talk about false vows, if it happens to be one who has offended them," replied his neighbor.

"You have little faith, then, in these holy brothers?" said Farel.

"Faith in them! who has in these days?" exclaimed the young man. "No, no; we are growing too wise now to believe in monks or priests, or anything they tell us. Let us follow our own reason, and enjoy life while we have the chance, for there is nothing for us after death."

"But judgment!" said Farel, solemnly.

"I don't believe that even, it's like all the other tales told by the Church. When we die there's an end of us. That's my *credo*," he added, laughing.

Farel shuddered at the levity with which this was said; and yet there was something winning in the

SURMOUNTED BY: *covered with*
CREDO: *set of beliefs*
LEVITY: *light-heartedness*

open honest face before him. "When we die we do but change the condition of life. Man's soul is immortal, and can never cease to live," he said.

"Well, I sometimes wish I could believe that," said the other, confidentially; "but when the priests trade upon the credulity of people, as they do, what are you to believe? What is truth? They have not a grain in their peck of lies. Religion is all very well," he went on; "it is a State necessity, I daresay; a means of keeping people down, governing them. But no one believes in it, or anything else, in these days; for those who know best about it, live most contrary to what they teach—the priests, and monks, and bishops, and abbots."

Guillaume Farel could not deny this; and what could he say to prove that this wholesale adoption of infidel opinions was an error as great as that of the Church in believing every delusion, and far more baneful in its effects. Certainly it could not be done here in the crowd; and so Farel asked the young man to come to his rooms, and discuss the matter with him there.

"I will come," he said; "but I warn you I shall not believe in your Church again. Rudolphe Mans, here, has tried to bring me back once or twice; but I cannot believe in a religion that gives a rich man license to do as he will, so long as he pays the Church liberally."

Rudolphe shrugged his shoulders and smiled. He was a rich man, and for enjoying every pleasure;

CREDULITY: *willingness to believe or trust*
INFIDEL: *unbelieving*
BANEFUL: *harmful*

he was of the same opinion as his companion, but he differed with him in believing that this life was all he had to consider. There was another life beyond the grave; but the Church would take care that he had the good things of that world, as well as this, if he only paid well for them, and believed all that was told him by his confessor. He could not say all this for the priests and ecclesiastics had passed, and now came the heavy tramp of archers, billmen, crossbow-men, and culverin-men.

It was nearly an hour before the whole funeral procession had passed, and Guillaume Farel was able to cross the road. Rudolphe Mans seemed as anxious to reach the old gabled house, and about equally disappointed. He looked at Farel and laughed. "We can neither of us speak to the girl, she has gone," he said, looking round among the crowd, who had begun to stir.

Farel's face grew dark. "What girl do you mean?" he asked.

"That is what I should ask—what do you mean by coming to seek this girl—this Marguerite, I think she is called?"

Farel could scarce restrain his anger, as he said, "And why do you seek her?"

Rudolphe only answered with his habitual shrug of the shoulders. Farel did not press him further, for he wanted to make sure whether it was Marguerite Leclerc he had seen standing here. There was no trace of them now; but people's tongues were

BILLMEN: *soldiers armed with bills, or long poles with curved blades attached to the end*
CULVERIN-MEN: *soldiers armed with muskets*

going fast enough about the young monk falling from his place in the procession; and by listening to scraps of conversation, and the comments of those who saw the whole affair, he very soon heard the true story of it. A poor woman standing in the front, had rushed forward as he drew near, and threw her arms around his neck, when he had pushed aside his cowl, and with the cry of, *"Mother!"* had dropped senseless in her arms. The poor woman's shrieks had attracted the attention of the whole cavalcade towards the spot, or it might have passed almost unnoticed.

"And where is the young monk now?" asked Guillaume Farel, of one who had stood near, and watched the whole proceeding.

"I know not; but he would be conveyed to the monastery with all speed, I should think," answered the man.

"Nay, but they could not take the woman to the monastery; and she would not be parted from him, thou knowest," said another.

"And this poor woman was his mother," said Farel, beginning to hope that Claude might not be dead after all.

"She must have been, or she would not have dared to bring such a scandal on these holy fathers, as to suppose they had human feelings."

"It was the mother's heart in her that cried out at the sight of her boy," said another woman, compassionately.

An Unexpected Recognition

"And that same mother's heart will bring sore trouble upon her, I doubt not."

"But can you tell me where this poor woman and young monk have gone?" asked Guillaume Farel, rather impatiently.

"Who helped to carry him when he was lifted up? He was a tall man, I know," said the gossip.

"'Twas an armorer, I think, by his dress," said someone standing near. "All was hurry and confusion. No one could well see what happened; and the archers made it worse by driving everybody back, monks and all. All I know is that a big armorer made his way through the crowd, carrying something wrapped up in a monk's dress, with the women fainting, and the men fighting all about him."

"Could it be Frollo?" said Farel, half-aloud, as he elbowed his way along towards the Petit Pont.

All the shops on the bridge were closed today; but the different signs by which each was known could be plainly seen; and conspicuous among these was the "Golden Lance," the sign above Frollo's shop.

As Guillaume Farel knocked at the door, and listened for some sign of the inmates being at home, he thought he could distinguish the sound of a door closing inside, and pieces of armor being moved, before the heavy bars were lifted down from the street door.

Frollo's face underwent a marvelous change when he recognized his visitor. "Monsieur Farel,

INMATES: *residents*

you are welcome," he said. "I had not thought to see you today; I feared it might be one of the brothers from St. Germain l'Auxerrois."

"And why should you fear a visit from them today?" asked Farel, looking at him curiously as he passed into the darkened shop. A small lamp stood on the counter, and its rays were reflected from various pieces of bright armor; but there was nothing particular in the appearance of the shop such as he had expected to find; and Madame was sitting in the inner room, working at her distaff, with Babette.

"There is nothing to fear," said Frollo, as he entered, closely followed by Farel. Madame immediately rose, and put down her distaff. Farel noticed that Babette looked very pale, and that there were traces of tears on her cheeks.

"Monsieur, we have a visitor," said the armorer, as his wife moved towards the door.

"It is Claude Leclerc, is it not?" asked Farel, anxiously.

Madame paused, and turned pale. "I told you he had been seen, that everybody knew this," she said, in a tone of alarm, speaking to her husband.

"Nay, I know nothing but that a young monk fell senseless to the ground today; and 'twas said his mother was in the crowd, and rushed to him. I should not have thought of Claude, but I saw his mother standing just where this happened, and on inquiry found that an armorer had helped to carry him out. There are many armorers in this city, and I scarcely dared hope it was you who had rescued him; but I came to see."

"And no one but yourself knows that you have come to the Petit Pont in search of him?" asked Frollo.

"No one," answered Farel.

Frollo looked greatly relieved. "You may come and see him," he said; "I will not venture to bring him to this room again." As he spoke, he was removing several suits of armor, which he laid down with as little noise as possible; and then, having done this, he touched a spring, and opened a sliding panel, which disclosed a flight of stairs. After descending these, another door was opened, and they entered a small chamber, where, on a wooden couch, lay the prostrate figure of a young monk. By his side knelt an elderly woman, whom young Farel recognized at once as the widow Leclerc; and at the foot of the couch stood Marguerite, her eyes red with weeping. The widow looked round sharply as they entered, and put her arms around Claude, until the armorer told her who it was, when she started to her feet, and fell on her knees before Farel.

"Oh, sir, you are rich and noble! save him, save my Claude! He is ill, he is dying; and they will take him from me again!"

"But that cannot be Claude!" said Farel, looking at the pale, emaciated face before him. The cowl

PROSTRATE: *laid flat*
EMACIATED: *wasted away*

had been pushed back, and the tonsured head, with its pain-drawn, weary face, could be plainly seen by the light of the lamp.

"Ah, you do not know him; but I was not deceived this time," said the widow, bending down and kissing that pale face.

His mother's kisses seemed to bring him back to consciousness again, and he opened his eyes, murmuring, "Mother! Marguerite!"

"Claude! Claude! is it indeed Claude?" exclaimed Guillaume Farel, bending down towards the bed. "Oh, Claude, let me tell you before you die that we have found it. Dr. Lefèvre has found 'David's Royal Fountain,' and all France will find it too."

Claude looked eagerly towards Farel. "You have found the Fountain!" he said. "Mother, lift me up,

TONSURED: *shaved*

I must live to hear of this;" and, by a great effort, he managed to raise himself by the widow's help. "Now tell me all you know," he said; but the effort had been too much for him. The next minute he fell back fainting in his mother's arms.

Chapter VIII

The Young Monk

G UILLAUME FAREL was greatly alarmed when Claude fell back in his mother's arms. "I have killed him," he said, wringing his hands, as he looked at the pale face before him.

Madame had brought some restoratives with her; and after the application of the unfailing burnt feathers to his nostrils, a little wine was forced down his throat, and he began slowly to revive. But Farel was still in great alarm. "A doctor should be fetched," he said.

But the widow shook her head. "Nay, nay; but they will carry him to the monastery," she said; "and I cannot part with him yet."

Frollo looked perplexed. "There are few who understand the art of healing save the monks," he said; "and they would not suffer him to remain here with his mother."

"There is Cop, the physician to the king's nephew—Francis of Valois. I will go and consult him," said Farel, after some little consultation with the

SUFFER: *allow*

armorer. Claude was sensible now, and looked anxiously after Farel as he left the room; but the presence of his mother and sister seemed to soothe him.

In the meantime Madame, with the help of Babette, brought various little comforts down for the invalid—some cushions for the hard wooden couch, and a thick coverlet to place over him, for the chamber was very cold.

As he revived, his mother ventured to ask him some questions, for she had not been able to hear anything yet. "Have you been ill long?" she said, tenderly.

"About a month, I think," answered Claude. "'Tis the wasting sickness," he said, holding up his long, bony hand.

"And you were out a month ago with a bag, begging for alms?" said the widow, tenderly.

"Mother, I saw you then, washing by the river; but I dared not speak, and drew my cowl over my face lest you should know me," said Claude, in an agitated tone.

"Ah! if you had but spoken I should have been content, and not have brought the scandal on you I have this day."

It was the first time the widow seemed to recollect what she had done. All her anxiety had been lest she should lose Claude again; but now an overpowering sense of the sin she had committed took hold of her mind, and she threw herself

SENSIBLE: *conscious*

upon the floor, and groaned in the anguish of her spirit.

Madame tried to raise the poor woman; while Marguerite went to her brother's side, and tried to soothe him; for his mother's distress affected him very deeply, and he had already suffered too much from over excitement.

"I wish you had spoken to Mother a month ago," she said. "Not being able to learn whether you were living or dead, we sent Fanchon to live at her aunt's; and Mother and I made our way up to Paris to seek news of you. We have had to get our living since then as washerwomen. When we saw you to-day, we were beginning to lose all hope, and made up our minds to go back home again. Mother's heart has hungered for you so much."

"Ah, Margot, not more than mine has, shut up in the monastery," said Claude, with a sigh. "And you ask why I did not speak? Margot, the brothers do not trust me; they have compelled me to become a monk; and I have tried to stifle all the love of my heart, but it will not die, and they know it—and so they do not suffer me to go in quest of alms without being watched."

Marguerite shuddered. "And they will take you away from us again," she said, the tears coming into her eyes as she spoke.

"Yes, I must go back to my monastery; but don't let them take me yet, Margot. I must talk to you and my mother and Guillaume Farel. He must tell me about 'David's Royal Fountain;' and I will carry the news of it back to brother Jacques, and then die. I am so old, Margot—my life has been such a long one."

He said the last words very dreamily, and clung to his sister, as if for protection, before he went to sleep. She looked at him and sighed; and then bent down and kissed him. It might be sacrilege to kiss him now that he was a monk; but she did not care. She only knew that her dearly-loved, long-lost brother rested on her arm, and she was ready to dare anything for his sake.

She repeated his words as she gazed at his shaven head, "You are so old, and your life has been such a long one! Oh, Claude, you are young yet."

"And I feel as though I were ninety," said the young monk, trying to smile. But it was so long since a smile had parted those thin lips, that it was a pitifully faint one, and the habitual look of meek endurance stole back again, as he gradually fell asleep.

Madame was in dire perplexity about the widow now. When Claude was carried into the house she had begged and entreated that they would conceal him, and not allow the monks to remove him from her; and now she was almost equally earnest in her beseechings to be allowed to go and inform the authorities at the monastery where he might be found. She had periled his soul, as well as her own, she said; and she must do what she could to atone

SACRILEGE: *stealing something sacred*

for this grievous sin, by giving him back once more to the arms of his holy mother, the Church.

Marguerite could hardly prevail upon her to wait until Claude awoke before doing this, so eager was she to set off.

Very fortunately, Farel returned while Claude was still sleeping. The famous physician had promised to come himself, and see the young monk that evening; for he had heard of him from Dr. Lefèvre, as well as Guillaume Farel, and felt some interest in his fate. By his orders some warm nourishing food was given to Claude, as soon as he woke, which he ate with evident relish, after a little persuasion from Marguerite; for he objected at first, saying he dare not break the fast that had been imposed on the whole brotherhood.

"But you are not in a condition to keep a fast," said Guillaume Farel. "You need strengthening and nourishing food now, or you will sink from exhaustion."

"Alas! you know not what you say," replied Claude, with a sigh; "it is only by keeping under my body, starving it into obedience, that I can ever hope to be a true servant of the Church."

"Claude, what do you mean?" asked Farel. "Do you think by starving yourself you will ever get rid of your sins?"

Claude shook his head mournfully. "I want to find the Fountain the monk of Clugny spoke of," he said. Then his face suddenly brightened, and he seized Farel's hand. "You said you had found this Fountain," he exclaimed. "Tell me, oh, tell me, can I find it too?"

Farel bowed his head, "Yes, Claude, it is ever open, ever flowing. We have but to open our hearts, and we shall receive its life-giving power. 'The blood of Jesus Christ cleanseth us from all sin.'" He repeated these words slowly and impressively, while Claude lay and listened eagerly to them.

"The blood of Jesus Christ!" he repeated; "and what else?"

"Nothing else," answered Farel; "we do not need the good works of saints or angels."

"Only our own," interrupted Claude; "and I have none to bring. I am constantly rebelling against the rules of the Church; and it is only when I am weak and subdued that I am obedient."

"But you need no good works to recommend you to the favor of God," said Farel, quickly. "The Lord Christ is waiting to be gracious, is longing to give you pardon, and assure you of His loving favor towards you."

Marguerite and the widow listened as attentively as Claude, and seemed much more able to take in the meaning of his words. The mind of the young monk was worn and enfeebled by disease; and it seemed that his spirits had been completely broken by the long-continued severities practiced upon him, and by him, so that he was quite unequal to the mental effort required to understand all Farel sought to explain. The words of Scripture had, however, taken deep hold of his mind, and he murmured over again and again, "The blood of Jesus Christ cleanseth us from all sin."

Soon after nightfall the physician came, as he had promised, bringing with him various drugs and decoctions, as well as precious stones, to be worn as amulets while the sickness lasted. He was a man deeply learned in Greek and Hebrew, and considered a most skillful physician; but some of his prescriptions would greatly surprise us in the present day. But his decoctions of herbs and insects did Claude no harm, if they did him little good; and being supplemented by good, nourishing food, and kind, careful nursing, he soon began to improve in health and spirits.

It had not been easy to induce his mother to allow the physician to attempt to cure him. She wanted to have him taken back to the monastery at once; and it was only on the physician telling her that the excitement of such a removal would probably cost him his life, that she consented not to betray his hiding-place. That she should not be suspected of concealing him, it was of course necessary that she and Marguerite returned to their work the following day; but Claude did not suffer by the exchange of nurses, for the armorer's wife, assisted by Babette, was unremitting in her attention to him.

It soon became evident that a frequency of fasts and unwholesome food was the chief cause of his illness; and Farel could understand what he meant

DECOCTIONS: *extracts obtained by boiling down*
AMULETS: *charms against evil*
UNREMITTING: *constant*

now by saying good food made him disobedient. It was only by a system of semi-starvation that they had been able to subdue his spirit at all; and now that he was getting stronger again, his hatred of his vocation revived in all its force.

It was, however, with joy and reverence that he listened to the wonderful truths taught by Dr. Lefèvre. Farel was scarcely less earnest than the professor himself in disseminating those truths. Many an hour was spent in the secret chamber under the armorer's shop, where he had not only Claude, but his mother and sister, as well as Frollo, and his wife and daughter, to listen to the wonderful story of God's free grace and love. These visits of the widow and Marguerite had to be made at night, for fear they should be watched by the monks, for they had heard that anxious inquiries had been made concerning him. The widow herself would have been relieved if his place of concealment had been discovered; but Guillaume Farel had taken upon himself the direction of affairs, and she dared not offend him, although her mind was tortured by the thought of the sin she was committing in not disclosing all she knew.

Her only satisfaction at this time was, in receiving Claude's repeated assurances that he would return to his monastery as soon as he was well enough to walk there. Against this young Farel could say nothing: he dare not teach rebellion against a parent's authority, even in such a matter

DISSEMINATING: *spreading*

as this. It was one of the fundamental principles in which a child was educated at this time—reverence for the lightest wish or word of either mother or father. Would that it had survived to our own day. It would be better for France, as well as for England, if it had. Possibly, if Claude and Farel had been left to themselves, the young monk would have broken his monastic vows by fleeing from Paris, and resuming his former occupation, at a distance; but now there was nothing before him but the unloved, unloving life of a monk.

It was some time before Farel could understand how Claude had been induced to take the monastic vows. But when he came to think of all Claude had told him, he could no longer wonder that his ardent, impetuous spirit broke down, and that in his bitter despair, he yielded himself up to the will of these holy fathers.

As Jacques had told him, Claude was detained in the schoolroom one afternoon, and was taken by the monks into the monastery. He never entered the schoolroom again, never saw one of his young companions, until Jacques entered the monastery as a monk, a few months previously. All this time he had been shut up within the walls of his gloomy prison, until at length, health and mental strength gave way under the slow agony he endured. He was, at the same time, diligently plied with those arguments, or rather sophistries, which Roman ecclesiastics know so well how to use. His superstitious

ARDENT: *passionate*
PLIED: *pressured*
SOPHISTRIES: *false and misleading arguments*

fears were worked upon. The love he bore to his mother and sister were appealed to; and he was told that by breaking the vow his mother had made of him to the Church, he would involve her in the curse he would bring upon himself; whilst by becoming a monk, he would work out her salvation, as well as his own.

Unable longer to resist the importunities and threats of the superior, Claude professed as a monk; and after awhile was allowed to take the monastery sack, and go out in quest of alms, when who should he see among the Seine washerwomen, but his own mother. She had come from Dauphiny in search of him, he knew; but he dare not speak to her—dare not let her see that he recognized her, for a spy was set to watch him. He staggered home, hardly able to bear the sack, which was little more than half-filled with the broken meat and vegetables he had gathered on his round; and almost immediately afterwards, he was seized with what he had called the "wasting sickness," which confined him to the infirmary for some time. As one of the choir, it was necessary that he should attend the queen's funeral; and he might have performed his part, and gone back to his monastery without anything happening, if it had not been for the meeting with his mother. This second encounter was too much for his feeble strength, and the excitement had brought an immediate relapse.

IMPORTUNITIES: *persistent demands*

Now, however, he was likely to be better and stronger than he had been for some time, for no expense was spared, either by Farel or the armorer, in getting him nourishing food—a thing that had been considered quite unnecessary for him by the holy brothers.

That he was not very anxious to go back to the monastery, can be easily imagined; but the thought that he could now carry with him the light of this wonderful gospel, taught by Farel and Lefèvre, reconciled him somewhat to that return. He knew that several of the younger brothers were, like himself, dissatisfied with the rites and ceremonies of the Church, and longed for something they could not find in them—pardon and peace, which only faith in the atoning blood of Christ can bestow.

The infidel opinions he had professed to believe in when he first came to Paris, had long since been abandoned; but he had not become perfectly reconciled to the Church. Now, however, his soul had found rest. Farel had opened his eyes to see and understand that "David's Royal Fountain" would not only "purge every sin away;" but that, by the teaching of the Spirit of God, this love would enable him to do the work of a faithful teacher, and thus the light of the glorious gospel would be spread throughout the length and breadth of the land.

It was a sorrowful parting that took place between Claude and his friends, when the day of his departure arrived; and from none did it cause him such a pang to part as from Babette. He had never forgotten her kindness to him on the night of his arrival in Paris; and now that they had sat together, listening to the teaching of Farel, and helping each other to a clearer understanding of these wonderful truths, it seemed to him that she was dearer even than his mother and sister. But this secret had to be carefully buried. By and by it must be fought against and conquered, but burying it was all Claude had strength for at present.

Some alarm was felt at first, lest the authorities of the monastery should punish him for his absence. But after a little time he was again seen going his rounds, with the sack, in quest of alms; and so these fears were relieved, and the widow looked more content than she had done for years, now that she had once more seen her son.

Chapter IX

Changes

It was a year of changes for France—this year of grace, 1514. Queen Anne died in February; and, in the following May, her eldest daughter was married to the heir-apparent, Francis of Valois.

Nothing could have pleased the Parisians better than this wedding, albeit they might have preferred its being postponed a little longer; for the court, being still in mourning for the queen, there were few festivities on the occasion. Francis himself might have preferred waiting, for he was not very deeply in love with his bride, but his mother, Louisa of Savoy, was extremely anxious for the match, and possessed such unbounded influence over her son, that he was guided almost entirely by her and his sister Marguerite, the young duchess of Alençon.

Gossip was rife about this among the students of the Sorbonne, but they rejoiced at the turn political affairs were likely to take. No one felt more interest in the revival of learning, and the success of

RIFE: *widespread*

the new doctrines, than Francis and Marguerite; and though the duchess of Savoy was too much occupied with her own pleasures and ambitious schemes to give much attention to literature, she loved her children too well to thwart them in what she considered a mere amusement.

The hearts of Lefèvre, Farel, and other earnest-minded men beat high with hope that the Church would soon be purged of all her errors, and send forth bands of teachers who should preach Christ and His everlasting gospel, instead of the fables and miracles set forth in the Breviary for the instruction of the people.

Though the present king, Louis the Twelfth, would not hinder this Church reform, they could scarcely hope that he would help it forward actively. But what might not be accomplished if the handsome, gentle, learned Francis came to the throne! And that he would succeed his uncle had been long predicted. It seemed inevitable, now that the queen had died leaving only daughters; for it was scarcely likely that Louis would marry again.

This was the popular opinion in Paris; and Guillaume Farel, with one or two companions, were discussing this one evening as they returned from the Sorbonne, when an acquaintance met them.

"Have you heard the news?" he added, almost breathless with excitement; and without waiting for an answer, he exclaimed, "The cursed English will not make war upon our France again!"

"Why, what has happened!" asked two or three
in a breath, for news from the seat of war was at all
times acceptable.

"The English are beaten at last. Our troops have
landed on their shores, and burnt their towns, and
will soon have conquered London and the whole
country."

Farel looked as though he somewhat doubted
this wonderful success; but Rudolphe Mans came
up soon afterwards: he had obtained particulars
of the whole campaign, he said, and the news was
quite correct. All the city went wild with delight
that evening; for the news spread like wildfire, and
orders were issued for public rejoicings to be cele-
brated the next day.

But the morning light brought news that greatly
diminished the joy of the citizens of Paris. Their
countrymen had certainly landed on the English
coast, and burnt the little town of Brighton, and
ravaged the Sussex shore; but they were not likely
to reach London, and dreadful reprisals had already been effected by the English, for they had
ravaged Normandy, and burnt several towns and
villages.

Rudolphe Mans looked sadly crestfallen when
he met Guillaume Farel a few days afterwards; but
it did not prevent him communicating his latest
piece of news.

"There is to be peace now with England," he
said, in a dissatisfied tone.

REPRISALS: *use of force to pay back for damages suffered*

"It were well if that peace were never broken again," said Farel; "love of war is the bane of our country."

Rudolphe shrugged his shoulders. "We shall never be at peace long with our old foes, the English," he said. "You do not ask either what is to be the price of this boasted peace," he added.

"We shall have to give up Brighton, I suppose; for we could hardly expect to hold it," said Farel, carelessly; for his mind had turned to another subject now, and he wondered why Rudolphe so often came down to walk near the sheds of the Seine washerwomen. He had not forgotten their encounter on the day of the Queen's funeral. But Rudolphe's next words put all other thoughts far away.

"You have not heard the talk about the King's marriage, then?" he said.

"King Louis' marriage?" exclaimed Farel.

"Yes! He is to marry this English princess, Henry the Eighth's sister," said Rudolphe.

Farel laughed. "That is like your news of the taking of London," he said; "and now I must ask you why you so often come this way to walk," he added, seriously.

Rudolphe started. "I may walk where I please, without asking the leave of the Sorbonne," he said, in a haughty tone.

"Certainly; but, Rudolphe Mans, I give you a word of warning."

BANE: *destroyer*

Whatever the warning might be, Rudolphe did not wait to hear it. He plunged into a cross street, leading direct to the Petit Pont; and Farel took the way leading to the poorer part of the city. He had made up his mind to pay a visit to the widow Leclerc, and persuade her, if possible, to return to her native province. Paris was no place for Marguerite and Fanchon, without the protection of a father or brother; and of course Claude was of no use now.

He found his task less difficult than he supposed. The widow had been puzzled at so often meeting Rudolphe in the street and at church; but his evident devotion while there had disarmed her of all suspicion, and she was inclined to be angry with Marguerite when she refused to go out alone. Now, however, she was as anxious to return to Dauphiny as she had been to leave it.

So she readily acquiesced to Farel's plans for her speedy departure from Paris. The season of the year was most favorable for traveling now, and the widow had nothing to detain her but her clinging love for Claude. Guillaume Farel promised her that she should have another interview with her son before her departure; and he went to the Petit Pont to consult with Frollo on this latter part of the arrangement. He would need the help of the armorer in carrying this out; for he wanted to see Claude himself, and inquire how the new doctrine had been received by the monks.

To his surprise the armorer met him with the same news that Rudolphe had. It was confidently asserted that the king was about to enter into an arrangement to marry the princess Mary of England, and thus secure a lasting peace between the two countries. Farel was unwilling to believe it; but the report was confirmed when he reached the rooms of Dr. Lefèvre, whom he went to visit afterwards.

The professor appeared quite depressed this evening; for he, like many others, was looking to the patronage of Francis to secure the adoption of the new opinions in France; but if the king married again he would possibly not have the power to aid them.

All doubt as to the truth of the report was soon set at rest. The peace was concluded in August; and then the king set out for Blois, to be betrothed by proxy to his youthful bride, who, with her train of English ladies, would shortly afterwards sail for France.

All Paris was astir with this news, when a young monk paused at the door of the armorer's shop one evening, and carefully looked round to see that he was not watched, before venturing to enter. Frollo was on the watch for him, and friends were waiting his arrival in the secret chamber below. The widow Leclerc and her daughters were to leave Paris the following day, and it was the last time they might ever see Claude; so that the mother's anxiety, lest

BETROTHED BY PROXY: *engaged to be married, where one or both parties might not be present, but instead send an authorized representative to complete the agreement*

anything should hinder his coming, may be easily imagined.

Guillaume Farel was somewhat disappointed to hear that Claude had been forbidden to speak of the new doctrines to the other monks. He had thought that they had but to be made known, and they would be eagerly received by all; but the superior of the monastery had declared them to be dangerous, and now Jacques, to whom Claude was most attached, had refused to listen to anything he might say on this matter, or even talk about the monk of Clugny's hymn, which they had so often sung together.

Poor Claude was looking sadly depressed and worn again now; and when his mother and Marguerite had taken their departure, he drew his cowl over his head, and buried his face in his hands, that no one might see the misery depicted there. Guillaume Farel was deeply touched, yet knew not how to comfort him; for it was indeed a sore trial he was called upon to bear. At length, however, Claude was able to speak again, and then he told Farel he expected to be sent on a preaching tour shortly. It was thought he would do less harm among the ignorant and unlearned people, than among the monks, who, having nothing else to do, were ready—some of them, at least—to take up any new doctrine, and to follow any false teacher. What Claude had said already, had been sufficient to induce some of the younger brethren to seek out the copy of the Holy Scriptures, hidden away in the library of the monastery; and they were now daily studying the Word of God—a study the superior could not forbid, although he did not like it.

Farel was glad to hear Claude was to leave Paris for a time; and that he might more clearly understand the new and glorious doctrine of justification by faith, he gave him a copy of Lefèvre's *Commentary on St. Paul's Epistles.*

As he walked home, thinking of Claude, he could not help praying that God would raise up many others to go forth and preach this truth; for he did not doubt but that the humble young monk would be the means of leading many to give up their dependence on saint and image worship, and trust in Christ alone for salvation. Humble instruments like this might accomplish much; but Farel hoped more from the patronage of the great and noble; and very soon the thought of the king's approaching marriage pushed other less important events out of his mind.

Nothing occurred to prevent the marriage, which took place at Abbéville about two months after the betrothal; and then all Paris was thrown into a ferment of preparation for the coronation, which was to take place at St. Denis on the fifth of November.

Whatever the doctors of the Sorbonne and Louisa of Savoy might feel, they dared not show anything but gladness, although all the hopes centered in Francis might be cut off by this English girl of eighteen. But Francis himself quite forgave his youthful aunt when he saw her, and publicly paid her and her favorite maid of honor, Lady Anne Boleyn, every attention.

The princess Mary's retinue became her state as the King of England's sister and the future Queen of France; but nothing went so far in overcoming the prejudices of the people, as her gentle, modest bearing, which was in striking contrast to that of Louisa of Savoy. The rather free manners of the French court somewhat astonished the English ladies, who found far more congenial companions in the wife and sister of Francis, than in his mother.

Frollo was busy enough preparing for the coming tournament, which was to last over a week. Many French and English knights would enter the lists, and contend for the prizes to be bestowed by Queen Mary and the young Duchess Marguerite. Madame Frollo, too, and Babette had their share of work in preparing the braveries—sewing on silver lace, and embroidering velvet surcoats with various devices.

But this outside work was not suffered to hinder that silent hidden work begun by Dr. Lefèvre at the Sorbonne, and now going on in so many hearts in Paris. Frollo had given up his indiscriminate gossip, and now he might often be seen in deep and earnest conversation with those he had formerly

RETINUE: *group of attendants*
BECAME HER STATE: *was suitable for her rank*
LISTS: *an enclosed area for combat*

encouraged in their bold and reckless doubts of the existence of God. He was eagerly looking for another visit from Guillaume Farel now; for his business had compelled him to travel to Meaux, and there he had met Claude Leclerc, who was laboring earnestly among the woolcombers of that city, and the peasants of the villages around; and thus doing the work of a pioneer of that gospel that was afterwards to find so many earnest adherents in this spot. But Farel did not visit the Petit Pont for some time. His attention was given almost wholly to the study of the Greek and Hebrew Scriptures; and, like a good soldier, he was preparing for that warfare he would so soon be called to enter upon.

Frollo was rather surprised, and a little disappointed, at not seeing young Farel; but he was not alarmed, for Madame and Babette frequently saw him at church, although the loud voices, interminable chantings, and words spoken without understanding by the people, who knew nothing of the language in which they were uttered, made him often sigh for a more pure and enlightened worship; and he longed for the time when the whole congregation should join in the worship of God with the heart and the understanding also.

One day Babette came home in a state of great agitation. She had gradually left off worshiping the images of saints and the Virgin; but she never passed a cross or an image of the infant Jesus—

DEVICES: *decorative designs*
INDISCRIMINATE: *careless, thoughtless*
INTERMINABLE: *endless, monotonous*

and this was the form in which He was usually represented—the Child, subject; the Mother, all-dominant—without bowing and generally kneeling to repeat some prayers. She had done this with many others at the church after *vespers*; and Guillaume Farel, standing in the crowd, had raised his eyes above the image, and exclaimed in a loud voice, "Thou alone art God! Thou alone art wise! Thou alone art good! Nothing must be taken away from Thy law, and nothing added. For Thou alone art the Lord, and Thou alone wilt and must command."

"And what said the priest?" asked her father, quickly. He was afraid the young student's impetuosity would carry him beyond the bounds of prudence, and he already foresaw trouble and opposition from the priests and monks.

"He did but look surprised, my father," answered Babette; "but I could not kneel longer even to repeat my prayers, for it seemed that Monseigneur Farel would have us pray to God Himself, without images as without saints. My father, is it so?" she added.

Maître Frollo sighed. "Would that I could read the Scriptures myself, and know of a surety what God would have us do in this matter."

"But our professor reads it," said Madame; "and we may surely trust him and the noble Monsieur Farel."

"And he says that the Scriptures expressly declare that 'God is a Spirit, and they that worship

OF A SURETY: *for sure*

him must worship him in spirit and in truth,'"[1] said the armorer, musingly. "I wish I could see this Holy Bible for myself," he added.

"My father, could they not print this Holy Bible at the new printing-presses?" asked Babette, eagerly.

"I doubt whether the king would allow it," answered Frollo. "If the learned and gracious Francis of Valois were king, he would aid in this good work, I doubt not." He little thought how soon he would be king.

The wedding festivities were scarcely over before the health of King Louis began to fail; and on the first of January, 1515, a herald issued from the palace bearing the woeful tidings that he was dead. In the Place de Grève, at the gates of the Sorbonne, in the flower-market, and on the steps of Nôtre Dame, did he with sound of trumpet proclaim, "Louis the Twelfth, the father of his people, is dead!" in the ears of the sorrowing citizens of Paris, who loved their king and deeply mourned his loss.

[1] JOHN 4:24

Chapter X

Babette, a Scholar

A YEAR or two has passed ere we again take up the thread of our story—years wherein the new doctrines, preached by Lefèvre at the Sorbonne, have spread quietly but surely, taking possession of many hearts. Guillaume Farel is now a doctor of that renowned University, and has even gone beyond his master in the boldness of his declarations against the errors of the Church of Rome. Lefèvre constantly exhorted his disciples to search the Scriptures for themselves, to make that Book their chief study; and Farel, with two brothers, Arnold and Gérard Roussel, had taken his advice, and were now eagerly proclaiming the liberty of the Gospel.

Not only the Sorbonne, but the court of France, was listening to these things now; and Farel and Lefèvre might often be seen wending their way to the Hôtel de St. Pol, or the Place des Tournelles, when their duties at the Sorbonne would permit.

This evening, there was a gathering at the palace,

WENDING: *making*

for the duchess Marguerite de Alençon, and her brother, Francis the First, were expecting a visit from the noble and learned Bishop of Meaux, William Briçonnet, and Farel and Lefèvre had been asked to meet him.

The brother and sister stood close together, engaged in earnest conversation. Marguerite wore a hood, or *coif*, of black velvet, ornamented round the forehead with a crimson band, studded with jewels, which completely hid the luxuriant masses of golden hair, but could not conceal the sweet grave face that so greatly won upon all beholders. Her two maids of honor, Lady Anne Boleyn (who had been transferred to her service since the death of the late king), and Lady Chatillon, evidently had been discussing Marguerite's dress; for the crimson satin robe was looked at with rather angry glances by the two ladies, as though they would fain have had their mistress dress with more care than had been bestowed on its arrangement this evening. To the critical eyes of these ladies the square-cut bodice, with its embroidery of gold and precious stones, was a little awry, and the rich lace of her hanging sleeves was not adjusted to their liking; for the fact was, Marguerite had been in such haste to meet her beloved brother that she had been very impatient in the hands of her tirewoman.

Francis looked every inch a king as he bowed to his sister; and then, dispensing with courtly

TIREWOMAN: *lady's maid*

phrase, kissed her white forehead, and led her to a seat, murmuring as he did so, *"Ma mignonne Margot!"* He was dressed in a habit of pale lavender silk, lined with green satin, and confined round the waist with a green girdle. He, too, wore a cap of velvet, ornamented with the same device as his sister's—a sprig of fleur-de-lis.

The two ladies in attendance upon Marguerite drew near to their mistress, when she had taken the seat of honor to which her brother had led her; and the king's confessor, and a young noble, Berquin, who were in attendance upon Francis, took their places behind his chair; and soon afterwards their visitors began to arrive.

The bishop came first; but he was almost immediately followed by the professor of the Sorbonne, and Guillaume Farel. Courtly distinctions were, as far as possible, dispensed with at these meetings, and Francis usually addressed these learned men as "My children."

This evening the latest news from Germany occupied Lefèvre's mind. The Pope had been put to a great deal of trouble by an ignorant, factious monk, Martin Luther, who was loudly protesting against the sale of indulgences, and preaching doctrines contrary to those of the Church.

Francis and the bishop had likewise heard of this, and severely censured the Elector for not putting a stop to the schismatic; but Lefèvre was not so sure that Luther deserved this name. He

MA MIGNONNE MARGOT: *My sweet Margot*
HABIT: *robe*
FACTIOUS: *divisive*

might be overbold, perhaps, in what he said; but it seemed there were strong points of agreement in their teaching, although the monk of Germany had probably never heard his name, or even that of the Sorbonne itself. He might have read the Word of God; and the same Spirit who had opened his eyes to the truth, might have revealed it in a like manner to Luther. At all events, Lefèvre would not condemn him until he had heard more of his doctrine.

The bishop was struck with the manner in which Lefèvre spoke of this Word of God. He did not refer to the Church and its laws and canons for his authority; but it was the Word of God—the Scriptures of the Old and New Testament—that he constantly referred to, when questioned by Francis and Marguerite on the subject of the new doctrines, and the liberty he declared the gospel gave to every man to serve God according to his own conscience.

This doctrine of liberty was the one most pleasing to the king and his courtiers, many of whom openly denied the existence of God when by themselves, although they professed to share in all the sentiments of Lefèvre. Just now he was in high favor, and the Reformed opinions were fashionable. But men refused to reform their evil lives, and conform themselves to the stern purity of the gospel, although they were ready enough to join in the cry for liberty of conscience and Church reform.

INDULGENCES: *forgiveness for sins*
CENSURED: *reprimanded*
SCHISMATIC: *someone who is spreading division*

All, however, were not alike. William Briçonnet was desirous of becoming a true and faithful bishop and shepherd of souls. With the docility of a little child he followed the advice of Lefèvre, and set himself diligently to the study of God's Holy Word. Through this, with the help of Lefèvre and Farel, he soon embraced, and resolved to teach and frame his life according to, the gospel of the grace of God.

Marguerite, too, among her ladies and the attendants and governesses of her little cousin, princess Renée, endeavored to promote not only a love of learning, but a love for this Word of God and the Savior whom it reveals. The learning, beauty, and grace of this illustrious lady gave her immense influence, not only with her brother, to whom she was very strongly attached, but also with the whole court of France; so that whatever Madame Marguerite chose to patronize, was at once taken into favor by the great and learned.

The humbler followers of Lefèvre thought there was little cause for fear now. Frollo was waiting in patient hope, believing that he should yet see a French New Testament; and Babette was learning to read from a clumsy-looking book her father had borrowed, for books written in French were very scarce in those days. Reading was not considered a necessary accomplishment for girls of the middle class, for they could scarcely hope to get books to read in their native language. Latin was

DOCILITY: *willing obedience*
FRAME: *pattern*

the almost exclusive language of literature.

A poor scholar who had come to Paris as penniless as Claude Leclerc, was teaching Babette to read; and she soon made such progress under his instructions, that she was able to spell out some of the satires that were published on the clergy. But her father was by no means so desirous that his daughter should read these as he had once been; and one day, while Babette sat at the table with her young instructor, Frollo suddenly exclaimed, "The duchess Marguerite de Alençon reads Latin they say, and Madame de Soubise is teaching the young princess Renée; so why should you not learn too, my Babette?"

Babette stared; but the young scholar rubbed his hands delightedly. "Mademoiselle shall learn," he said, without waiting for her consent.

"You will try, my daughter," said Frollo, looking at her anxiously. "I am getting an old man, or I should set myself to master these letters," laying his hand on the book, and looking at it with a puzzled face. Frollo had often blessed the Virgin and all the saints, that he had had nothing to do with witchcraft and reading; but those days had gone by now, and he sighed as he wished he was a few years younger, that he might set himself to the task.

Babette had wondered that her father wished her to learn to read at all; but that he should wish her to learn Latin seemed past belief. "My father,

I am not a princess, but a poor burgher maiden," she uttered, in her surprise.

"You are not a princess, but you are a woman, Babette; and why should you not learn this Latin, if I wish it?" said her father, severely.

"Nay, nay; but Latin is not for women," said Madame, who had just entered the room in time to hear her husband's last word. "'Tis the language of the Church, as you know; and 'tis not meet that ignorant women should pry into all the holy mysteries of our religion."

"'Twere better if the language of the Church were that of the people," said Frollo, impatiently.

Madame looked shocked at this bold speech; but her daughter's words horrified her still more. "I should like to know the meaning of all that is said in Church," she exclaimed. Madame lifted her hands and shrugged her shoulders as only a Frenchwoman can, but it was enough to deter Babette from saying any more. Frollo, however, was determined to carry his point.

"It were well if you and all women—ah, and men, too—understood the language in which they worship God," he said. "'Tis to me passing strange that such meaningless service should be more acceptable to the Lord Christ than words spoken with understanding; and I have had my doubts of late whether this is not another device of the pope's, to keep us in ignorance of all things that concern us."

MEET: *appropriate*
PASSING STRANGE: *extremely strange*

"That cannot be; for 'tis but a year or two since the great council was held at Rome, when the Holy Father declared the Church to be both pure and prosperous, and needing no reform," interrupted Madame.

Frollo rose from his seat, and walked out of the room. This Lateran Council and its decision was a never-failing bone of contention between the armorer and his wife. Madame declared that the Pope and council must be infallible in their decision; which, considering that she believed every priest and monk to be the same, was not saying very much for his holiness, and the divines who had met with him to consider the state of the Church, and congratulate each other upon the fact that "darkness covered the earth, and gross darkness the people."[1]

"If these bishops and abbés were taken up less with their pleasures they would know more of what is going on in the world," said Frollo to his apprentice, as he passed into his workshop.

The young man raised his head, and looked at his master in some surprise, for Frollo was usually very cautious in speaking of such things; but he was thoroughly roused now. "Gaston," he said, "you are an apprentice, and may live to see strange things in this city of Paris; but I am an old man, and can scarce hope to see more than the dawning of the light. God is about to renew the world, and you will see it. These dumb dogs

---

[1] ISAIAH 60:2
INFALLIBLE: *free from error*
ABBÉS: *abbots*

of bishops cannot see the great changes working in the hearts of the people, and so they have declared all things are well with the Church, and there is no need of reform; whereas if there be no reform in her, she is even now tottering to her fall."

Gaston looked at his master as if doubting his sanity, and then, hastily crossing himself, muttered over some words to be used as a charm against the spells of witch or wizard. He had begun to suspect before that his master had something to do with the black art; but he was sure of it now, or how could he predict what would take place after his death. The stalwart apprentice positively shivered with terror as he thought of this, as his master went out of the room again. "Maître Frollo a magician, an astrologer," he murmured; "who would have thought it? I hope—" But here he left off his self-communing to listen to what his master was saying to Babette in the adjoining room.

"Babette, I desire that you will apply yourself with all diligence to learn this Latin language, in which most of the new books are written," said Frollo. "I have heard that the learned professor of Rotterdam, Erasmus, has published a New Testament in this language, and I would have you read it, my daughter."

If Frollo had turned his head he would have seen his apprentice listening to all that was said; but with such a look of horror in his face, that he could not go on with his work.

STALWART: *strong, sturdy*
SELF-COMMUNING: *talking with himself*

"So Mademoiselle Babette is to learn to read these strange books, that she may be a witch," he murmured, as he again crossed himself. It needed no great effort to hear what was passing in the adjoining room, for the door stood halfway open, and Frollo was close to it.

"Mademoiselle will learn to read the Latin very quickly," said her young instructor; "but, but—" and here he hesitated, and looked doubtfully at the armorer.

"What would you say?" asked Frollo, encouragingly.

"Is it possible for you to get this New Testament of Erasmus?" said the poor scholar.

"I think so," replied the armorer; "but why do you ask?"

"Because I greatly desire to see this book for myself," replied the lad; "I met with a young monk near Meaux, when on my way to Paris; and he said this New Testament was the very Word of God, and taught the way of eternal life more clearly than did the priests or monks."

"A young monk preaching near Meaux," repeated Madame; while Babette colored, and looked eagerly at the lad.

"Yes! He said the blood of the Lord Christ would wash all our sins away. I shall never forget this part of his sermon," said the poor scholar; "for he was so earnest, and begged everyone to believe what he said, that Christ alone, and not the priests, could forgive sins."

"'Twas Claude Leclerc, I doubt not," said Frollo.

Babette did not speak, but her cheeks glowed and her eyes sparkled, as she bent over her book, and said quietly, "My father, I will learn this Latin, as you desire."

"And I will buy a New Testament at once," said Frollo; "and our poor scholar here shall read from it, and expound its meaning to us."

This arrangement pleased the lad; but it was evident that Madame was somewhat doubtful about it. "I doubt whether it is for women and unlearned men to know what is contained in the Scriptures," she said.

"But it is God's Word spoken to man," said her husband, a little impatiently.

"Ah, but not to unlearned men," said Madame, shrugging her shoulders. "If it were for men at all it is only for doctors and professors, or the Pope and priests; and I greatly fear that evil will follow if we be guilty of the sin of bringing such a book into this house."

Frollo saw they were likely to get upon the troublesome subject of the authority of the Church again; and thinking it were better to leave things as they were, without provoking further resistance, he returned to the shop, leaving Babette to her reading, and Madame to work off her fears at the ends of her distaff.

A few days afterwards Frollo brought home a large parcel; and, when it was opened, a rather clumsy-looking book was lifted out. Madame

EXPOUND: *explain in detail*

crossed herself, and bowed in reverence before it, but positively declined to hear it read. Whatever she might believe of the new doctrine taught by Farel, she would not compromise her soul's safety by reading the Scriptures for herself; and so, when the lad arrived, who was to read the New Testament, she went up to her oratory to intercede with St. Catherine for her husband and daughter, that no evil might follow the bold step they had taken in daring to read God's Word for themselves.

Chapter XI

The Arrest

JT was late at night, and the Seine crept lazily under the bridges of the city, looking black and murky where the light fell upon it. There were few lights to be seen now, except from the windows of the Palace and the Hôtel de St. Pol, and a few of the larger mansions of Paris; for all the shops were closed, and there were few people abroad, except the city guard and a party of halberdiers, who were making their way to the Petit Pont.

One or two people who happened to be looking from their windows before they went to bed, saw them pass, and wondered what could have happened. But they did not trouble themselves to do more than this; and when some others heard the rattle of weapons on the stones, and the hammering at the door of their neighbor the armorer, they only shrugged their shoulders and exclaimed, "Frollo has offended some of his troublesome customers, the students of the Sorbonne, and they are going to give him a fright."

HALBERDIERS: *soldiers armed with halberds, long poles with ax blades and spikes on the end*

The armorer himself was just putting away the New Testament when the first knock was heard; and thinking, like his neighbors, that it was some of his troublesome customers from the Sorbonne, who had just discovered their lack of some bravery for their comedy, and come to supply it, he did not hurry himself; but quietly bade Babette go upstairs to her mother, and saw the poor scholar to his little slip of a room at the side of the shop.

But before this was done there came a tremendous hammering at the door, which somewhat roused the armorer's anger; and as he pulled back the heavy bolts, he said, "How now, messires, would you beat in the door of an honest man?"

A stout-built, surly-looking halberdier stepped forward, and seized Frollo's shoulder the moment the door was opened. "You are my prisoner," he said, with a sort of suppressed growl.

The armorer looked at his captor, and then at the rest of the band. "And so this is part of your comedy-play tonight, messires," he said; "you have come to seize Frollo the armorer."

The man stared. "By St. Louis, you are more likely to find it a tragedy than a comedy, my man," he said, handing Frollo over to the care of one of his men, while he passed into the back room. Babette's book lay on the table. "Thanks to our Lady, I know nothing of this pestilent reading which, it seems, must always lead to witchcraft," he muttered, as he laid his sword across the book, and began to make further search about the room.

PESTILENT: *harmful*

Frollo was in doubt now whether this arrest was a joke or a reality. He resolved, however, to treat it as a joke, until convinced that it was grim truth, and so he said, "Hold there, messire student, do not be too rash in thy handling of my wife's distaff."

A low growl came from the captain within the room. "If thy wife and daughter had kept to the distaff, and thou to the fashioning of armor, the stone-cage would not be troubled with thee," he said.

Frollo started slightly. What had he done to bring this visit? He did not ask this question aloud; but warning one of the men not to tarnish a bright steel chain coat with his flaring torch, he again called to the captain: "Come, tell me of what I am accused," he said, trying to speak lightly.

"Information has been laid against you at—"

A growl of displeasure came from the captain; and at the same moment the frightened faces of Madame and Babette were seen in the little doorway leading to the staircase. Babette gave a slight scream as her eyes fell upon the halberdiers; but Madame asked, in a shrill, sharp tone, what they were doing. She evidently took them to be riotous students, as her husband had done, and was by no means disposed to be too civil to them in this character. In her fine white gorget and petticoat of tiretaine, with red and blue stripes, Madame did not look a woman to be frightened at the sight of a sword or halberdier; and yet, as she gained a nearer view of the intruders, her face grew whiter even than Babette's.

GORGET: *a scarf-like covering for a woman's neck*
TIRETAINE: *a cloth woven with wool and linen*

The Arrest of the Armorer

"I have no orders to take you womenfolks as yet," said the captain, as he came out of the room, thrusting Babette's book into his leathern pouch as he spoke. Madame's first thought was that her husband was arrested for theft; but when she saw this she hastened to explain that the book had been borrowed of a neighbor. Writing, like reading, was not one of the captain's accomplishments, or he might have written down the name and address of the owner of the book, for he was very particular in asking it, and repeated it more than once, that he might not forget it.

"But you will not take my husband now," said Madame, attempting to go to his side as she spoke.

But she was roughly pushed back as she did so. "Keep off, he is my prisoner," growled the captain; and turning to his men he said: "To the Tournelle;" and at the name of the prison Madame screamed as loudly as Babette had done.

The halberdiers, quite used to women's screams, marched their prisoner off between them; while Frollo was so overcome with the suddenness of the whole affair, that he walked between his captors without asking a single question, or making the least resistance. Resistance certainly would not have been of much use, for it might have brought the dangerous-looking weapons by which he was surrounded down upon his head, and saved the trouble of a trial; for they were rough times of which we write, and a life more or less in the State was not thought much of. So through the dark, silent streets of Paris, tramped the armorer a prisoner, not knowing of what he was accused, and not likely to know until he was brought to trial.

Madame and Babette, with the poor scholar, who had crept from his hiding-place as soon as the soldiers had left, sat up half the night, asking each other this puzzling question, and of course quite unable to find an answer; only Madame protested, in a complaining tone, that it was all caused through the new learning and printing presses, which were an invention of Satan to lead men away from the Church.

In the morning Gaston came, and grew pale as he heard of his master's arrest. "What did they say when they came," he asked, in an alarmed tone.

Madame shook her head. She could not speak now; but Babette seemed disposed to take her mother's place, for she was by far the most calm. "We do not yet know of what my father is accused; but you will give all diligence to the shop, while my mother goes to the Palais de Justice this morning."

Madame left off crying to look at her daughter in surprise. "Babette, what are you saying?" she exclaimed; "I was never at the Palais de Justice in my life."

Babette colored. "Nor was my father at the Tournelle before," she said; "but he is there now, and we must know whereof he is accused. Pardon, my mother," she said, kneeling down at her feet.

"I have been overbold in speech perhaps," she added.

Madame rocked herself helplessly to-and-fro. "These new ways will teach maidens to be bold, I trow, or you would not so forget yourself, Babette, as to ask me to go to the Palais de Justice," she said.

"Nay, my mother, I would spare you this. If you will, I will go and ask the president whereof my father is accused," said Babette, gently.

Madame gave a faint scream. Had Babette proposed climbing to the highest pinnacle of Nôtre Dame, she could not have looked more alarmed. "Ah, me, but evil times have fallen upon the world when a maiden could propose this to her mother. No, no, Babette you must not leave me. We must wait, and perhaps we shall hear by and by."

But Babette was by no means disposed to wait, or to depend upon the chance rumor, brought to them by some neighbor, whose curiosity might lead him to the Palais this morning. "My mother, we must do something," she said; "my father is helpless, and—"

"Yes, yes, we will do something," interrupted Madame, impatiently. "If he had but been a true son of the Church the saints might help him; but he never was, Babette, never," said Madame, impatiently; and she began to cry again.

Babette had not much faith in the saints or the Virgin either; and so she ventured to suggest that Gaston should be sent to inform some of their friends what had happened, as her mother declined to go to the Palais de Justice.

"But who shall I send for?" asked Madame. It was plain she had begun to depend upon her daughter, although she had resented her suggestions. Before Babette could name anyone, however, Gaston came to say that a monk was in the shop, asking to see Madame. She, however, declined seeing anyone just now, and Babette went instead; while Gaston busied himself in dusting and arranging the armor and various weapons hanging about the shop.

The monk glanced at him suspiciously from under his cowl, and pointed towards the room door as though he wished to speak to Babette privately. The girl took the hint; and with a lowly reverence, thinking it was her mother's confessor, she said: "Holy father, will you walk in, and speak a word of comfort to my mother, for she is in sore trouble this morning."

Gaston looked almost as suspiciously as the monk had looked at him, when he saw him enter the room, followed by Babette.

The girl closed the door as her mother rose, and bowed her head to receive the holy father's blessing; but instead of extending his hand in the customary form, the monk raised it, pushed aside his cowl, and disclosed the pale, worn face of Claude Leclerc.

Babette started; and her cheeks grew crimson

as she dropped upon the oak chest standing near, and the young monk was no less agitated. "Babette, forgive me for coming near you," he murmured, in an undertone, as Madame rocked herself backwards and forwards, groaning helplessly. "In that other world, which is a home and not a monastery, I may see and speak with you without sin. Oh, Babette! Babette! the misery of being a monk," he groaned; and then he resolutely turned his back to her, and went to Madame.

"You would ask for my husband," she said, through her tears; "but he is not here—he is in sore trouble, and neither you nor the saints can help him."

"I do not think the saints can," said Claude, quietly; "but the Lord Christ will, I trust; and I have come to tell you what will be best to do that he may not be condemned for this crime."

"What crime?" asked Babette, breathlessly; "we know not whereof my father is accused, as yet."

"And you will not know until he is brought to trial; but I strongly suspect that it is for witchcraft."

"Witchcraft!" uttered Madame, with a shriek. Murder was accounted a less crime in those days, and so her alarm as to the consequences of this charge was not groundless.

"Witchcraft!" repeated Babette, with ashy lips, and starting to her feet. "Oh, save my father! save him, save him!" and then she fell senseless at the monk's feet.

Madame was in a state of consternation and bewilderment that made her almost incapable of doing anything.

"Gaston! Gaston!" she called; and in a minute or two the apprentice came, staring and gaping, into the room, as the monk passed out.

"What is it?" he said, changing color a little, as he noticed Babette's pale face.

"I don't know. Fetch some burnt feathers, and run for the neighbors," exclaimed Madame, hardly knowing what she said in her fright.

"More witchcraft!" muttered Gaston, as he ran through the shop to perform his mistress' last command, as being easiest to perform.

It was not long before help arrived, and Babette was carried upstairs and laid on the bed; but the neighbors were not slow in condemning the monk's unfeeling behavior in leaving two helpless women alone in their trouble.

The poor girl slowly revived; but as her eyes opened, they wandered from her mother's face in search of another, and she said, in a trembling whisper, "Where is he? My father, what of him?"

Madame started. She did not care to let the neighbors know the dread charge on which her husband had been arrested; for they would undoubtedly be afraid to come near them, or even enter the shop, lest the articles sold should be infested with magic; and so, laying her hand upon Babette's shoulder, she said: "You must not talk

CONSTERNATION: *alarm and dismay*

now, my dear. I will send Gaston to the Palais de Justice, and doubtless he will bring us news."

Babette understood her mother's motive for wishing her to be silent, and did not speak again; while a confused buzz of whispering went on around her, for some had not even heard of the arrest of the armorer until Gaston came to fetch them, and all wished to hear a detailed account of it from Madame herself. The recital seemed to do her good; and on Babette declaring that she felt better, and only wanted an hour's sleep to make her quite well, she proposed to go down to the shop, while she sent Gaston to the Palais de Justice to hear what he could about his master.

One of the gossips offered to stay with Madame Frollo for the rest of the day—an offer which she gladly accepted, but which almost made Babette groan as she thought how helpless this would render her in doing anything for her father at present. Something must be done, she knew, and that very quickly, for he might be brought to trial that very day; and it was to think about this, and devise some means for helping him, that she wished to be quiet just now.

But when her mother and their visitors had gone downstairs, and only the splash of oars in the river below was heard, mingling with the confused hum of the noise in the streets, her thoughts flew towards Claude Leclerc, and his words, "Heaven is a home, not a monastery;" and it took away a great dread that had been growing upon her of late, whenever she thought of Claude; for if heaven was what she had hitherto supposed it—a monastery and nunnery on a large scale—how could she ever go there, and meet Claude without sinning, as she did now whenever she thought of him, seeing he was a monk.

Now, however, she lost sight of his sacred character, and thought of him only as her father's helper; for she believed he would help him if help would avail; and with the restful thought that Claude was even then seeking out the best means to deliver her father from this impending calamity, she fell asleep, breathing a silent prayer—not to saint or angel, but to the Lord Jesus Christ Himself, that He would help and deliver them in this great trouble.

Chapter XII

Tried for Witchcraft

THE trial of Frollo the armorer did not take place until nearly a fortnight after his arrest; and the particular crime for which he was imprisoned had not been made known, except as Claude had divulged it on the morning of his visit. Nothing had been seen or heard of him since at the Petit Pont; but Guillaume Farel had paid a visit to Madame, and said he had seen Claude, and been informed by him of what the armorer stood accused. Of course he would befriend him as far as possible; but even learned and enlightened men in those days believed more or less in this witchcraft, and so it was not surprising that Farel should look grave and serious when he spoke of this charge.

It was a weary time of suspense for Babette and her mother; and when the day of trial came at length it was almost a relief. The large hall of the Palais de Justice was spacious and gloomy, and looked still more so to Babette, who had come with her mother to hear all that was said. At the

A FORTNIGHT: *two weeks*

further end was the raised platform for the Judges; on the right and left of these the counselors in their black and red gowns. But it was not the sight of these that struck such terror into the crowd, as it came pouring in at the low door, and paused for a minute to look round; but on the left sat a grim figure in black, that was more dreaded on a trial than all the murderous-looking pikes and halberds that could be got together; for this was the king's attorney of the ecclesiastical court, and when he appeared with his officials it was known that the prisoner would be tried as a sorcerer.

Babette shivered with an undefined dread when she saw this official, and understood who he was. Until this moment she had indulged a slight hope that Claude might have been mistaken in his supposition; but there was no room for this any longer. After a few minutes of bustling by the crowd, another door at the side opened, and, guarded by a double line of pikes and halberds on each side, the prisoner slowly advanced to his place.

Frollo's head was bowed, so that his face could not be seen; but his whitened hair bore testimony to his sufferings. Babette clasped her hands, and Madame uttered a suppressed groan, as they noticed this. But there was another prisoner, it seemed, for the door did not close at once, and the pikemen still kept their places. In a minute or two another made his appearance, tottering between two jailers; but whether his feebleness arose from age or

PIKES: *long spears*

infirmity it was difficult to tell. His dress was of a nondescript character, neither lay nor clerical; but he wore no cowl on his bare head, and whether it had lost its natural covering from age, or the tonsure, was a point debated by the crowd. He was accommodated with a seat, for he seemed quite incapable of standing; and the other prisoner was noticed to start when his eyes fell upon his companion in misfortune.

Babette had caught a glimpse of this second prisoner as he came in; but she only saw a bent, feeble, bald-headed man. All her interest was centered in her father just now, and she waited impatiently for the trial to begin.

She did not have to wait long. The clerk of the court called her father's name, to which a hollow voice was heard to reply; and then followed another: "Claude Leclerc, formerly a monk of the monastery of St. Germain l'Auxerrois."

"Here is the wreck of Claude Leclerc—all that his brother monks have left of him, I suppose— but without life enough even to answer to his own name," said a clear, strong voice, that could be heard by almost everyone in the room.

A shudder ran through the whole audience that was not officially connected with this trial, and the crowd swayed to and fro in its eagerness to catch a glimpse of the bold speaker. Babette, however, only clasped her hands the tighter, and bowing her head to hide her frightened face, said in a low tone

OF A NONDESCRIPT CHARACTER: *of no particular type*
LAY: *of the common people*
CLERICAL: *of the clergy*

of suppressed agony, "Oh, merciful Lord Christ, spare him—spare him—and my father too!"

Madame was kept up as much by the fear of the crowd discovering that she was the prisoner's wife as by anything else. The dread lest the cry should be raised, "A witch! a witch!" and she should be hunted out, bewildered her so much that she could not attend to any of the preliminaries, and only awoke to the reality by a loud voice calling, "Gaston Ledru!" Babette started as she heard the name, and crept closer to her mother, as she saw their apprentice walk up and take his place. He was the principal witness, it seemed, for the officials of the ecclesiastical court at once proceeded to examine him. His examination occupied some time; but the evidence he gave was quite conclusive to those who had made up their minds about the verdict before a word had been uttered. To them it was clearly proven that this Frollo was a sorcerer, wizard, astrologer, and had many dealings with the prince of darkness, or how could he tell his apprentice what would happen years after he was in the grave. It was well-known that he had little love for the Church, or any of the holy fathers, except as he could bewitch them with his sorceries, and by that means bring them under his power.

A short speech to this effect, by one of the officials, was made to serve as the opening of the monk's trial; when it was shown that Claude had given himself up to the delusions of this Frollo some years previously; that the sorcerer had miraculously carried him away from a procession going to St. Denis on the day of the late Queen Anne's funeral, and that he was not heard of for several weeks afterwards. On his return to the monastery he had said he was taken ill, and carried away insensible; but his neglect of all the holy duties of a monk, his horror of holy water and all sacred relics, and his refusal to worship the saints, or even the Holy Mother herself, plainly proved that he had been under satanic influence. This neglect had been going on ever since; and in spite of the tender warnings and admonitions of the superior, the monk had continued obstinate, until at last it was deemed necessary to deprive him of all holy offices, and hand him over to the secular arm.

This last act of pretended mercy was the merest farce; for it was well-known that in all cases of witchcraft it was the spiritual rather than the secular power that was to be feared.

Although the trial took place in a public court, everyone felt certain that condemnation would follow this speech; and the judge was about to rise and pronounce the sentence, when a loud cry was raised by someone: "A witness for the accused; a witness for the accused!" and at the same moment a young man, in the dress of a doctor of the Sorbonne, stepped forward and announced his name, "Guillaume Farel."

INSENSIBLE: *unconscious*
OFFICES: *positions*
MEREST FARCE: *a total mockery*

He gave a brief, clear account of the connection of Frollo and Claude, and narrated the circumstances which had happened on the day of the queen's funeral, showing there was no magic or witchcraft in the case, but merely an act of kindness on the part of the armorer; and concluded by offering to call Cop, the king's physician, to prove the truth of his statement.

The effect of this plain, common-sense account of the miraculous carrying off of the young monk, was almost magical in its effect upon the crowd. More than one among them had heard this story before, and one man standing near Babette, called out aloud that he had seen the whole transaction.

The authorities on the left were plainly growing uncomfortable at this unexpected turn in affairs; but they were not to be put down by it. Rising from his seat, one of the officials announced that the charges had not yet been completed against the prisoners; and he then went on to state that the armorer Frollo, not content with practicing strange arts, did likewise read divers strange books not written in mortal language, and also that he compelled his daughter to do the same, to the end that she might become a witch.

Gaston again came forward to witness to this; and Babette listened with a thrill of horror, as he detailed the conversation he had overheard respecting her learning Latin, that she might read the New Testament of Erasmus. The name of the

DIVERS: *various*

language, as well as that of the book, was carefully suppressed, however, and was merely spoken of under the vague name of "strange," which, to the ignorant portion of the crowd, meant supernatural. This second part of the charge against Frollo evidently caused some sensation in court; for the crime of compelling a young girl to become a witch was held to be something horrible in the extreme, and again the judge rose to deliver sentence.

Babette, panting, breathless with excitement, saw the movement, and, moving from her mother's side, she shrieked, "Stop! stop! I must speak first—I am the girl."

"A witch! a witch!" was passed from lip to lip throughout the crowd; and Babette found that a passage was soon cleared at her approach, for all dreaded to come in contact with even the hem of her tiretaine petticoat. The excitement took away all fear of consequences, as well as natural timidity; and she pressed up to the barrier that separated the crowd from the official part of the court, and then exclaimed, in a tone of trembling eagerness: "I am Babette Frollo."

"And you deliver yourself up as a witch," said one of the officials on the left. "You confess the crime of which your father stands accused, and desire to be reclaimed from the power of Satan, through the merciful dealings of our holy Mother Church."

Babette glanced at the crushed form of Claude

as a proof of the "merciful dealing" she might expect; and the sight of that bowed figure, and her father's whitened hair, nerved her with courage to say in a clear, loud tone, "No, I am not a witch. My father sought to lead me in the path of light, and not darkness; and the language he desired me to learn was the Latin tongue, wherein the mass is performed, and in which all the prayers of the Church are uttered."

The judges and counselors looked amazed at the bold speaking of the girl. "Do you know that girls have no right to learn Latin?" said one of them, impressively.

"My father believed I could and ought to learn it if the Duchess d'Alençon and the princess Renée did," answered Babette.

Several laughed at the idea of a bourgeois maiden comparing herself with these high personages; but the counselor frowned, and said, in a stern voice: "Tell me now, girl, wherefore did you learn this Latin tongue? Was it not enough for you that the priest understood the words of the mass and prayers?"

"Pardon, seigneur; but I wanted to know what the words meant that I so often repeated in the *Ave* and *Credo*, and—and—" and there Babette hesitated, remembering that the Testament had been carefully concealed by her father.

"Go on, go on," said the counselor, thinking that the girl would be betrayed into speaking

CREDO: *the Apostle's Creed, an early formal statement of Christian beliefs*

Tried for Witchcraft

of some wrong use that had been made of the Latin.

"My father desired me to learn Latin, that I might read the new books, and especially the New Testament," said Babette, in a lower tone.

Again there came a frown on the faces of the ecclesiastical portion of the judges, and an angry whisper was heard to pass: "More of this pestilent monk's doings."

It seemed there was a difficulty now in passing sentence on Frollo, for the charge of witchcraft could not be maintained against him; and it was not yet a crime, according to law, for a person to read the New Testament. But as the monks had, for purposes of their own, connected him with the charge against Claude Leclerc, they resolved that he should not escape.

At this moment a letter arrived from the king, commanding that sentence should be deferred until he could himself inquire into the case. Everybody was astonished except the doctor of the Sorbonne, Guillaume Farel; and he knew that the powerful influence of the king's confessor and physician had been gained on behalf of the two prisoners by himself and Dr. Lefèvre.

But a serious difficulty now arose in the minds of the ecclesiastical portion of the court. Claude had been formally degraded, and deprived of all the offices and immunities which his sacred calling gave him, before being handed over to the secular power, so sure did his judges feel of getting him condemned; but now this letter of the king's upset their arrangement, and left him as a mere secular man in the hands of the civil magistrates.

Could he be reclaimed, and taken back to the monastery? They asked this question of each other in a whisper, glancing at the almost lifeless-looking figure before them. Had the case been heard in the hall of their own monastery they would have had might on their side. Taking the law into their own hands they would have speedily hurried him down to the dungeons below; but here the case was different. Their power was limited to a civil court, and there was always a latent jealousy of each other's rights. Such a case had never been known to occur before. There was still an old breach between their order and the Sorbonne, which it was not to their interest to widen. They therefore determined, should their claim be resisted by Farel, that the case of this degraded monk should be handed over to the Sorbonne, as the only means of getting out of the difficulty gracefully, and yet not yielding *their* prisoner entirely to the civil power.

So, as soon as Frollo was removed, the ecclesiastical officials came to take charge of Claude, but Farel at once interfered. "This is now a civil case," he said; "this man is no longer a monk—he has been degraded from his office; and the king's letter commands that *both* be committed to the care of the civil magistrates."

LATENT: *sleeping*

The counselor bowed blandly to Farel, and after asking a thousand pardons, said: "We deem not that the civil power hath the right to touch this man; and, therefore, waiving our claim to the recusant, we hand him over to the care of the most learned and holy Sorbonne, to be dealt with as shall be thought fit."

This the man thought would be sure to please one of its doctors; but, to his surprise, Farel looked somewhat dubious. The fact was he did not feel willing to establish any precedent for giving the University too much power. Just now it might answer very well, for the friends of reform were the most powerful; but, by and by, it might lead to bad results, if the other party happened to have the upper hand, as he often feared they would, in spite of the labors of Lefèvre and himself. So he said quietly: "It wert better to have this monk dealt with according to the civil law." But this they would not do; and so at length Claude was formally handed over as a prisoner to the Sorbonne, and the court broke up.

BLANDLY: *smoothly*
RECUSANT: *someone who is obstinate*

Chapter XIII

A Parisian Gallant

A PARISIAN crowd in the sixteenth century differed very little in its main elements from one of the nineteenth; and as the idle, chattering, gossiping mob poured out of the grand hall of the Palais de Justice, their tongues were busy enough concerning the strange turn events had taken that day. There was but one opinion among them about his Most Christian Majesty King Francis. He could do no wrong.

As he had decided that the trial should be adjourned, instead of there being a public spectacle at Nôtre Dame and an execution at the Grève, why of course it was right; more especially as the witchcraft had not been clearly proved.

This latter consideration was, however, of secondary importance to the minds of the crowd. The name of being a witch, or sorcerer, without anything being proved against the individual, was enough to lead to the stake but a short time before, and the dark ages were only just passing away.

It was during one of those transitional times, when light and darkness, truth and error, are so mingled that, in the words of the prophet, "it is neither day nor night."[1]

Learning was fast pouring its light upon the nations of Europe; but, with the taste for this, there still existed the knightly exercise and love of arms—and this, with an ever-increasing love of luxury and pleasure, prevented its taking any deep hold of the people as yet, and made them willing to leave the consideration of the more serious affairs of this life and the next, provided leisure was allowed them to enjoy themselves upon every possible occasion.

This trial of Frollo's was a little diversion to the idle gallants of Paris: a change from hawking and hunting—their favorite amusements; but they were a little disappointed that the second and third acts of the drama had been stopped, and grumbled accordingly.

Madame had stood in a state of suppressed agony while Babette was speaking, expecting each moment to find the crowd dragging her forward to answer to the same charge as that brought against her husband and daughter. But Babette was allowed to depart without further questioning when the king's letter had been read, greatly to her mother's surprise and relief, who contrived to meet her, and slip out as soon as the prisoner had been removed.

[1] ZECHARIAH 14:7

They chose the quietest and most unfrequented streets on their way home; for each moment they feared the cry would be raised by someone, "A witch! a witch!" and that they should be hunted through the streets of Paris until rescued by the guard and lodged in prison. The Petit Pont was reached at length, to their intense relief; and then they found that the shop had been left in the care of two halberdiers, who had taken possession when Gaston Ledru went to give evidence against his master, the armorer.

Madame stared and trembled a little when she saw the fierce-looking men. They were as polite as though paying a mere visit of ceremony, but none the less determined to retain possession; for, in point of fact, the judges had felt so sure of their condemnation of Frollo that they had sent to seize his property beforehand, knowing it would be forfeit to the State through this charge. Madame threw herself helplessly onto the oak bench when she reached the inner room; but this new aspect of affairs seemed to give Babette fresh courage. Learning to read for herself had helped Babette to think for herself; and she saw plainly enough that she would have to take care of her mother now, and not waste her time in useless lamentations over her father's fate.

But the first thing she did was to run upstairs to her little oratory, and kneel down to thank God for delivering her father, and ask His guidance, protection, and blessing for the future. Then she went down; and finding her mother still in helpless grief, resolved to speak to one of the halberdiers, and ask him how long they were likely to remain in charge of the shop.

The man opened his eyes at the simplicity of the question.

"By St. Louis, we shall not leave until—until—" and the man stopped, for he could not bear to tell this young girl that her father would be sure to be burned, and she and her mother turned out homeless and penniless, even if a worse fate did not await her.

Babette guessed, however, what was passing in the man's mind; and she said, in a faint, trembling voice, "My father's trial is postponed, and it is not certain that he will be condemned."

The man bowed. "Then Mademoiselle may sell as much as she pleases, until the matter is finally settled," he said.

Babette and her mother were very much at their mercy now. He and his men could have pillaged the house, and they depended for much of their pay on pillage, and on what they could exact from the citizens. So to them it was but a part of their trade to plunder all who fell into their power. His permission to sell what they could of the stock was, therefore, a most unexpected favor. Babette was not ungrateful. She begged that they each would choose a sword, or some piece of armor for themselves at once; and then went to consult her mother as to what would be the best thing to be done under these circumstances.

But Madame was totally incapable of advising anything. She could only throw herself helplessly at the feet of the Virgin, tear her hair, and ceaselessly repeat the Latin words of the Rosary, of which she knew not the meaning. Was it wonderful that from this meaningless exercise she could gain no comfort and no confidence?

Finding her mother unable to help her with the necessary arrangements for the business, Babette tried to persuade her to kneel down with her, that they might together pray to God in their own language, for His help and deliverance on behalf of their father and Claude.

But Madame put aside the suggestion as a temptation of the evil one himself. "No, no, Babette, it is this following our own judgment, instead of that of the Church, that has brought all this dire trouble upon us. If your father had but followed the teachings of the Church, instead of following his own understanding and reason, he would not have been suspected of the terrible crimes of witchcraft and heresy."

Babette was still vainly trying to console her mother, and wishing some friendly counselor would come to her aid when the door opened, and the young doctor of the Sorbonne appeared.

Guillaume Farel knew that without the friendly countenance of someone likely to influence others,

WONDERFUL: *surprising*

the poor family would be entirely forsaken at this time, and so he had brought with him an unwonted companion—Rudolphe Mans—one of the gayest gallants of the city; for he thought if they were allowed to sell any of the stock, Rudolphe might prove a profitable customer.

He had heard of the trial that day, but had no idea that the monk was his former companion, Claude, and he looked unusually serious when he heard it. "I always liked the poor fellow, in spite of his poverty and persistence in doing what he thought right," he said. "I knew it would bring him into trouble someday; for his code of rules differed from that of the Church, and was a great deal more troublesome. By St. Louis, I would not be plagued with such a religion as his for anything; 'twere better to be without altogether."

Farel shook his head seriously, and was about to speak, but Rudolphe exclaimed: "There, there, pray don't begin preaching to me. One of these holy fathers caught me the other day, and treated me to such a dose that I went straight off to my confessor, and got shrived without delay, though that was not quite what the monk had bid me do."

"What was this monk's command, then?" asked Farel, curiously.

"Oh, he tried to persuade me to use my learning in reading the New Testament there is so much talk about just now among your Sorbonne doctors; and, not content with that, I must frame my life according to its teachings, too," and the young man

UNWONTED: *unusual*
SHRIVED: *forgiven for sins confessed*

shrugged his shoulders and made a wry face, to show his disapproval of this.

"It was Claude Leclerc who spoke to you, I doubt not," said Farel, quietly; "and it is for teaching and preaching this truth of God that he hath so sorely suffered at this time."

"But he is charged with witchcraft," said Rudolphe, quickly.

"That is but an excuse to get him out of the way," said Farel, in a whisper; for walking here in the narrow streets leading to the Petit Pont, he might be overheard by someone passing.

Rudolphe stared. "I have heard queer tales concerning these monks," he said; "but I believed not they would proceed to downright cruelty against any."

"Nay, they would do anything to gain their own ends, I am well-assured now. I did not think so once; but this Claude and his strange story hath opened my eyes to see how utterly corrupt the Church is. Dr. Lefèvre hopes to see it reformed, and will not entirely leave its communion; but I am beginning to see that its rottenness lies at the very core, and that it must be leveled to the ground before we can hope to build another;" and Farel's cheek glowed and his eye glistened with repressed emotion, as he spoke.

His gay companion stared at him in amazement. "By the saints, you must be mad, monsieur," he said. "Would you cast away all your hopes of

escaping from purgatory by cutting yourself off
from the Church, just for a few cruelties that a few
monks may happen to practice on one of their
number."

"But it is not these few cruelties only," said Farel;
"and, besides, I doubt the power of the Church
to—"

"You must doubt everything then," interrupted
Rudolphe. "Is the Sorbonne going to dispute with
the Church the right of holding the keys of heav-
en?" he asked, in a slightly sarcastic tone.

"I do not think any Church or any power on
earth will ever hold them," said Farel, quietly.

The young gallant stared. "I am not learned in
these things," he said, trying to subdue his rising
anger; "but I have often heard the monks in their
sermons declare that to St. Peter was given the sole
power of opening or closing the gates of heaven or
hell, and this power has been transmitted to the
popes, his successors."

It was not pleasant for him to hear that the
Church which he had bribed to such an extent as
to cost him half his patrimony, was not in possession of this mighty power; and that, after all, he
might not escape the punishment due to his evil
life.

Farel guessed what was passing in the young
man's mind. "I know you are trying to get the best
of both worlds," he said; "but, believe me, it will
not do. For every evil work God will bring us to

PATRIMONY: *inheritance*

judgment; and the Church, by her masses and plenary and perpetual indulgences, cannot reverse that judgment."

Rudolphe looked uncomfortable. "I have always been careful to confess my sins to the holy Father Clement," he said.

"And why did you confess them?" asked Guillaume Farel, seriously.

The young gallant stared. "The Church commands it," he replied.

"The Scriptures also command it," said Farel: "but with this difference, that confession should be made to God, and the sin forsaken; whereas the Church holds out an inducement to continue in sin, by promising pardon on some payment being made, or some penance being performed. Is it not so? Have you not gone to confession to rid your mind of its catalogue of evil deeds, only that you may with more freedom and zest enter on another course of folly?"

Rudolphe could not but admit that this had often been the case. "But I have always been careful to attend all the festivals of the Church," he added.

"And do you think these few half-hearted services could atone for all your evil life?"

"I have no business to think about it," said Rudolphe; "it is just because men like you and Dr. Lefèvre refuse to follow the authority and judgment of the Church in all things, that these

PLENARY: *complete*

discussions arise that upset men's minds, and make them dissatisfied with what suited their forefathers. What business have I to question what the Church asserts? It's quite enough for me to pay the dues, and do her bidding. For the rest I am not responsible: it's her business to take care of men's souls, and see them safe into heaven; just as it is Frollo's to fashion chain armor, and temper sword blades; and I might as well question his right to temper and file them, as to doubt any of the means the Church follows to save me. All I have to do is to follow her bidding, and I can enjoy myself here and get out of purgatory too."

Guillaume Farel sighed. It seemed useless to try to convince such an one as Rudolphe; and as he thought of how many in this city of Paris lived and died with no better hope and trust than he had expressed, his face grew even more anxious. And yet, how was it to be altered? The Church taught false doctrines, but the people loved to have it so; and the only hope of escape was in pulling down the whole fabric, exposing its errors, corruptions, and falseness, that the people might no longer trust in its lies.

Unlike Luther, who built up as he pulled down, Farel thought only of the destruction of the stronghold of error and superstition. He was rather the forerunner than the reformer. Calvin was to do this work; but as yet his name had not been heard in Paris, and Farel was still hoping much from the

TEMPER: *harden by heating and cooling*

favor of King Francis, and his sister, the young duchess.

The conversation with Rudolphe had turned upon this subject before they reached the armorer's shop; and the young gallant had regained all his easy good temper as they stepped in and saluted Babette, who was still speaking to the halberdiers.

A look of pleasure stole into her face as she recognized the doctor of the Sorbonne; but she took little notice of his more gaily attired companion. The violet silk doublet, slashed with crimson, did not meet with much notice from her; but she hastened to ask Farel to step into the room, and speak to her mother. She hoped she should hear news concerning Claude as well as her father, from the doctor of the Sorbonne; but just as he had seated himself and spoken some words of comfort to Madame, she was summoned to the shop again, where she found a monk awaiting her, and Rudolphe Mans critically examining some fine steel coats.

Chapter XIV

At the Armorer's Shop

ABETTE was not without some apprehension when she saw that the monk wore the grey frock and rope-girdle of the order to which Claude belonged, and she trembled slightly as she bowed to receive his benediction.

Before bestowing it, however, the monk caught sight of Rudolphe, apparently for the first time; and, hastily drawing his cowl closer over his face, muttered the usual form of words in a low tone. He then gazed intently at Babette for a minute or two, and said slowly: "You have received news of a recreant brother of our order, one Claude Leclerc."

Babette stared, and was about to say that Dr. Farel had only just entered the house, and had not had time to communicate anything to them, when, recollecting herself, she said: "Nay, indeed, holy father, we have heard nothing concerning him, but what was spoken at the trial today. We know not even—"

"Peace, daughter," spoke the monk; "I have not come to bandy words with you; but to command

RECREANT: *cowardly, deserting*

you to tell me all you know concerning the ways and doings of this same monk."

"But you must know more of Claude Leclerc's ways and doings than this maiden can," broke in the customer; and at the same moment Rudolphe contrived to draw aside the monk's cowl with the piece of armor he was handling. "I thought I could not be mistaken in the voice," he said; "I thought I recognized Jacques, who was the former friend of this Claude Leclerc."

The young monk scowled at this interruption; but knowing the blind obedience his former schoolfellow yielded to the Church, he said in a tone of authority: "Hinder me not with vain questions, Rudolphe Mans," and he tried to draw his cowl over his head again. But Rudolphe had no intention of allowing this. He never had any love for Jacques; and his respect for the Church was not proof against the temptation of teasing him a little, in spite of his monk's frock and reputed sanctity. So he contrived to entangle the fastenings of the breastplate he held in the grey serge cowl, so that it was impossible for him to draw it on. "There is some danger in meddling with armorers, you see, Father Jacques," he said, giving the breastplate another jerk, so as to disclose the whole of the tonsured head.

The monk grew crimson with passion. "Rudolphe Mans, you will hear of this again," he said; "you show no respect to the holy order to which I belong."

SANCTITY: *holiness*

"Nay, nay, I bear every respect to the order; I am but wanting in it to you; and now I will ask what respect you had for poor Claude, when you laid information against him as a heretic?"

This was but a wild guess of Rudolphe's; but his words caused the monk to cease contending for his cowl, and turn pale. "How know you that?" he asked. Then turning towards Babette, he said: "It is through your witchcraft;" and in spite of the sanctity of his dress, the monk actually trembled at the sight of the girl; while she was not less frightened at the import of his words.

Rudolphe laughed, and determined to pursue his advantage. It would be something to relate to his companions, this baiting a monk in the armorer's shop, and he said, "Never mind how I gained my intelligence; but I know you watched him about the city, and carried tidings to the prior of every person he spoke to, and the words he uttered, and that was not all either, for *words* fail to dislocate bones, and—"

"Nay, nay, I had naught to do with putting him to the question," interrupted the monk, who, quite forgetting his errand to the armorer's daughter, was only anxious to escape from the shop now.

After a little more pulling and contending for the possession of the cowl, the monk was allowed to draw it over his head; and then he hastily retreated from the shop, while Rudolphe burst into a loud laugh at his discomfiture. The halberdiers, too, smiled grimly at the fun they had witnessed.

IMPORT: *meaning*
DISCOMFITURE: *confusion and embarrassment*

But poor Babette looked more frightened than ever. She knew it might be followed by serious consequences to herself and her mother; and what she had heard concerning Claude being put to the torture filled her heart with agonizing fears for him.

She took little notice of her customer; but hurried into the inner room as soon as the monk was gone, where she found her mother in tears, as usual, and Dr. Farel vainly trying to soothe her.

He rose from his seat as Babette entered. "What did the monk want?" he asked, somewhat anxiously.

"You should have begged the holy father to come in," said Madame, in a complaining tone.

Farel raised his finger, and repeated his question, adding, "You must be cautious, Mademoiselle, very cautious; for the life of your father, as well as of Claude, may be the price of any unguarded answer; and I doubt not you will be plied with many artful questions during the next few days."

"Nay, then, I will close the shop, and speak to no one before ascertaining their business through the wicket in the door," said Babette.

Farel smiled, but shook his head. "That will not do," he said; "you must try and sell as much as you can of your stock, for I greatly fear you will have to leave Paris if your father is released."

"Leave Paris!" repeated Babette and her mother, in surprise.

ARTFUL: *crafty*
WICKET: *a small opening*

"I greatly fear it, from what I have heard from Claude," said Farel.

Babette colored. "You have seen Claude?" she said, "oh, tell me how he is!"

"He has been put to the torture in the monastery," he said, slowly; "but it was not for the crime of witchcraft."

Babette had dropped helplessly onto the oaken bench, with clasped hands and pale face. "He has been tortured," she said, with a shudder; "tortured because he tried to teach men to trust in God, rather than the Church—to lead them to 'David's Royal Fountain,' he so often spoke of. Is it not so?" she asked.

"It is," said Farel, sadly; "and I know not whether he will recover from the injuries he has received. The King's physician has promised to see him to-night; but I greatly fear that some of his limbs are so far dislocated that he will never recover their use."

"Oh, say not so," exclaimed Babette, imploringly. "Doctor Cop is clever, as well as gentle; beg him to save him."

But Farel had turned, and was pacing up and down the little twilight room. "If Claude is to be saved, you will have to do it," he said, at length, pausing before her.

"Only tell me what I can do," she said. "I will do anything, if only I may hear that he is safe, and getting better."

"That I cannot assure you of at present; but

Monsieur Cop hopes something from the fact that the moon is as yet only in her first quarter," and Farel gazed at the pale crescent, now faintly showing herself in the sky.

Strange as it may seem to us now, the most implicit faith was put in the influence of the moon on sick people. Many sick persons lost their lives because friends and relatives thought it useless to apply remedies, when the moon happened to be on the wane at the time when they were taken ill.

After a few more turns up and down the room, Farel said: "Claude's life will not be safe in Paris, if he should escape condemnation, any more than your father's will; and so you must try to provide means for their safety, while you have the opportunity."

"What means?" asked Babette, eagerly.

"Money will be necessary, of course," replied Farel; "and to provide that you should sell as much as you can of the armor, taking a low price for it, to induce customers to purchase. And then I think a store of provisions should be secretly conveyed to the chamber below."

But at this Babette shook her head. "That is impossible," she said; "for the halberdiers would at once discover it."

"True, I had forgotten them," said Farel; "but still you must contrive to hide provisions in the house, for I fear there will be some difficulty in escaping from Paris, for Claude especially. But it

IMPLICIT: *unquestioning*

shall be done, if possible; and he shall leave the city a free man."

He did not wait to say any more; but passed into the shop, where he found Rudolphe well-nigh tired of waiting. He had pulled down morions and swords, chain coats and breastplates, by way of amusement. He had grown tired of this, and of joking with the grim-looking guards; but still he did not like to lose the opportunity of boasting to this doctor of the Sorbonne how he had baited the monk.

The sight of the arms and armor littered about recalled to Farel the purpose for which he had brought Rudolphe here, and assuming a gay tone, he said: "If you purchase all those things, no other gallant in Paris will stand a chance to get such a bargain."

Rudolphe glanced at the things scattered around. "There is one or two I should like, if Mademoiselle is disposed to sell them cheap."

"Mademoiselle will sell everything cheap now," said Farel; and as he spoke he slipped a gold crown into the hand of one of the halberdiers, for he knew it depended greatly upon them whether Babette sold her stock or not.

Babette had often been in the shop when her father or Gaston was serving, but she seldom served herself; so that she felt rather timid at bargaining with the gaily-dressed customer whom the doctor had brought. But Rudolphe was not disposed to be

MORIONS: *helmets*

hard; and before he left the shop he had bought several expensive articles, and promised Farel to tell his friends where they might suit themselves with similar bargains. He was very soon boasting to a little knot of companions how he had visited the Petit Pont, in order to satisfy his own mind whether Babette was a veritable witch, and how he had there met with a monk who was more frightened of her than he was.

Of course his companions were not to be outdone by this boasted bravery. They too, would go and see the little witch, and purchase some of Frollo's armor; for a bargain was loved as dearly in those days as it is now.

Babette had little time to spare for the indulgence of useless lamentations. Gaston did not make his appearance to assist her in the shop, and her mother was of very little use; so that she was compelled to take the whole management of affairs, for friends were shy of associating with those accused of witchcraft. But her labors in the shop did not absorb her whole attention. By sunrise every morning she was in the market, making purchases at the various stalls; for she had not forgotten Farel's injunction to lay in a store of food, and this could only be done by buying it in small quantities, at different places, for fear of arousing suspicion.

In this way another fortnight passed, ere the trial was resumed; but Farel had been as busy

VERITABLE: *true*
INJUNCTION: *instruction or command*

during that time on behalf of his friends as Babette herself. The king's physician had taken great pains with poor Claude's injured limbs; and, thanks to his remedies, or the moon's favorable influence, he was now so far recovered as to be able to walk to his seat without assistance, although both arms were still supported in a sling, and he looked pale and weak from intense suffering.

Babette and her mother were both present, eagerly watching for the appearance of the prisoners; and Babette closed her eyes, and murmured some words of thanksgiving when she saw Claude enter the hall unsupported. Her father, too, was looking better and more hopeful, she thought; and for herself she had quite made up her mind that he would be released.

The improvement in Claude evidently caused some surprise, and not a little consternation in the ecclesiastical conclave, more especially when an advocate stepped forward, and demanded, on behalf of the Sorbonne, that its prisoner should be tried in conjunction with the armorer simply as a layman, now that he had been degraded from all spiritual offices and privileges.

The monks saw they were likely to be caught in their own trap by this arrangement, and at once objected; but the advocate of the Sorbonne silenced them by saying that the doctors of the University had sat in judgment upon the case, and, confirming the sentence of the prior, had declared Claude

CONCLAVE: *an assembly of church officials*

Leclerc fully degraded and free of all vows taken previous to his condemnation; and, therefore, the ecclesiastical laws were no longer binding upon him further than upon any other layman.

This all seemed very uninteresting to the crowd; and was not heeded much by Babette, as it was only a quibble of law, she thought, and uselessly hindered the trial; but to the prisoner at the bar the declaration that he was a free man—free of those vows he had been forced to take, but in which he had no faith—was as life from the dead. His head was lifted, and a smile of hope beamed in his eyes, as he slowly turned towards where Babette was standing.

But the monks' double dealing ruined their cause this time. The crime of witchcraft had never been mentioned to Claude until he was brought forward in this public trial. He had been tried and condemned by a chapter of his brethren, for teaching views similar to those of Dr. Lefèvre and Farel. This had been mentioned to the king and duchess Marguerite, and their influence had been used on behalf of both prisoners.

In consequence of this the trial was soon over. Both were acquitted of the immediate crime of witchcraft, but condemned to seven years' banishment from the city and suburbs of Paris. Claude was so overcome when he heard his acquittal, and understood all that it meant for him, that he fell back fainting, and was carried out of the hall quite insensible.

QUIBBLE: *minor point*
CHAPTER: *an assembly*

Chapter XV

The Degraded Monk

LONG consultations were necessary to decide how Claude should leave Paris; for his friends judged and judged truly that the monks, disappointed of taking his life fairly, would leave no means untried of dispatching him secretly when he was on the road to Meaux, whither Frollo had resolved to remove his wife and daughter, as soon as the few effects he was allowed to have could be packed.

Frollo looked much more careworn than before he went to prison, and he could not but feel his losses severely; for he was getting an old man, and the hope he had indulged of passing the evening of his days in peace and comfort was at an end now. The loss of his business, and the expense of the trial, had well-nigh ruined him; and he would have to find some employment when he reached Meaux to support himself and his family, which was not a pleasant prospect for one who had prided himself on being a free burgher of the city of Paris.

DISPATCHING: *murdering*

But under all these trials, and the numerous slights and vexations to which he was now exposed, Frollo was calm and peaceful. He had learned in the prison what he had never fully learned before—to cast himself entirely upon the Lord Jesus for strength and salvation, and all that he needed for this life as well as the life to come. The instruction he had received from Guillaume Farel, and the teaching of Dr. Lefèvre, came back to his mind with fresh power, and he learned to rejoice that—

> "And David's Royal Fountain,
> Purge every sin away."

He did not know that it was because he was suspected of holding these new views, that such ready credence had been given to the superstitious fears of his apprentice; but Dr. Farel did, and he began to fear that the Reformed doctrine would not have such an easy triumph in France as he had hoped.

The syndic of the University, Noël Bedier, had begun a violent declamation against literature, against the innovations of the age, and against all those who were not earnest in repressing them; and having a greater veneration for the doctrines of the Church than the Word of God, he was transported with rage against all those who dared to differ from him. Lefèvre, Farel, and other learned doctors of the Sorbonne, who taught that the Word of God must be followed in preference to the Church, where the teaching of the two differed,

CREDENCE: *belief*
SYNDIC: *elected representative*
DECLAMATION: *speech*

were his special abhorrence, and Farel soon perceived that this adversary would stir up a persecution against them.

Under these circumstances he was anxious that Claude should be out of the power of the Sorbonne, as well as the monks; and so it was determined that he should once more take refuge in Frollo's house. But an unexpected difficulty arose when Farel mentioned this. Claude was very unwilling to go there.

The doctor stared: "You are a free man now—more free than you have ever been before. You have put away your vows with your monk's dress, and can choose your life as you will."

"I have already chosen," said Claude; "I will spend my life in spreading these new doctrines among the people—the poor and ignorant—who cannot hope to be able to read the Latin New Testament, or even the learned Dr. Lefèvre's works. I will tell them the joyful news that Christ died for sinners."

"And God will bless you in your work, Claude," said Farel; "but still I do not see why you should cut yourself off from all friendship. I thought you would have rejoiced at your freedom, and been willing to travel with Frollo;" and then he told him the fears that were entertained for his safety if the monks should discover him.

Claude had not thought of this, and for some minutes he sat in evident perplexity as to what

VENERATION: *respect or reverence*
TRANSPORTED: *carried away*

course it would be best to follow; but at length he said he would do just as his friend thought best in the matter. Traveling was often very dangerous in those days: the roads from one town to another were little more than mule or bullock tracks, or bridle paths, through miles of uncleared forest, where the wild boar and wolf roamed at pleasure, and they were often infested by men scarcely less lawless than these beasts of prey. It was, therefore, necessary for men to travel in company, unless it happened that they wore the dress of a monk or hermit, which was some protection from the robbers, and gained them admission at any roadside house or woodman's cottage on their way.

Claude had forgotten that he no longer possessed this protection when he proposed traveling alone, or that it was necessary for him to assume some disguise; but Farel was fully aware of the fact, and as soon as the darkness of evening fell, he set off to the house of Frollo with Claude, to consult upon the best mode of leaving the city. It was not easy to decide this. A monk had already taken up his position on the Petit Pont, commanding a view of the armorer's shop, doubtless for the purpose of giving his superior notice of all that passed. Farel had foreseen that this would probably happen; and it was for this reason he had told Babette to lay in a store of food; and he now advised that, as soon as all their preparations were complete, they should shut up the house and retreat to the secret chamber, where they could remain for a few days, and then, by the passages leading to the bank of the river, take a barge, and, following the course of the river Marne, reach in disguise the city of Meaux.

When these things had been discussed, Farel told his humble friends of some of the more public events that were likely to affect the progress of that gospel they had learned to love so deeply. He shook his head sadly when the armorer spoke of the certainty of its triumph here in Paris: he was by no means so sanguine as he had been a short time before. He was learning the wisdom of the exhortation: "Put not your trust in princes;"[1] for although the king, with his love of literature and learning, was willing to protect and encourage all those who protested against the darkness of error and superstition, he was by no means disposed to conform his life to the requirements of the gospel. He loved his own pleasures and despotic power, far more than he loved the truth of God. He had given fresh proof of this by the terms of the Concordat just concluded with the Pope. Parliament and the University alike, were resisting his will in the matter; but it was not difficult to see how the struggle would end.

Another influence was at work in this direction. The profligate and infamous Louisa of Savoy, the queen-mother, with her favorite, Duprat, upheld the King in his determination to carry this

[1] PSALM 146:3
SANGUINE: *confident*
PROFLIGATE: *recklessly immoral*

measure against the wishes of his people. Duprat was with the King at Boulogne when the Concordat was signed; and he had turned to his minister before putting his hand to the parchment, and whispered: "It is enough to damn us both." But this terrible thought had not hindered him from carrying out his project: he wanted money and the pope's alliance; and what was salvation to him, compared with these solid and present advantages?

All this Farel explained to his friends as he sat with them, bidding them not regret too much their enforced departure from Paris.

"The bishop of Meaux—Monseigneur Briçonnet—is doing what he can to reform and enlighten the clergy under his charge; and it may be that the gospel will make greater progress there, than here at Paris," he said, speaking as cheerfully as he could. He should miss these humble, faithful friends, he knew; and he could not help sighing as he spoke.

"And the Sorbonne, will it receive this Concordat peaceably, think you?" asked Frollo.

"No, no; neither the University nor the Parliament will submit to the king's pleasure in this matter without a struggle; for do you not see that the king, being so fond of pleasure and gallantry, the Church will be the means of rewarding his favorites; and it is well-known that the chancellor, Duprat, in his avariciousness, will himself take holy orders, that he may obtain some of these benefices."

AVARICIOUSNESS: *greediness*
BENEFICES: *salaries given to church officials*

"It seemeth that the Church is in worse case than ever, and I had hoped that the Lord was about to renew it," said the armorer, in a tone of consternation.

"Doubtless He will; but I fear it will not be by the hand of King Francis, as many hoped," replied Farel.

"And the queen-mother is said to have great influence with our king," said Frollo.

"Yes; but Madame Louisa, and her favorite, the chancellor, will join hands with Bedier, the syndic of the Sorbonne, against those who preach the gospel; for although she and her noble ladies may love to hear of its liberty, they love not to frame their lives according to its pure doctrines."

"Is everything so sad?" cried Babette; "has the noble Duchess of Alençon likewise given up her love for the truth?"

"Nay, nay, Madame. Margaret is still as warmly attached to Dr. Lefèvre and the gentle Bishop of Meaux as ever she was. She likewise is at great pains to instruct her maids of honor; and hopes that whenever the noble lady Anne Boleyn should return to her native England, she will carry the knowledge of the truth with her."

"And the little princess Renée, will she too learn to love this glorious gospel?" asked Babette.

"Yes, I doubt not but she will; for her governess, Madame de Soubise, is most diligent in studying Dr. Lefèvre's works, and the princess is most apt in acquiring every branch of learning."

"It was hearing that she had already learned to read in the Latin tongue that made my father wish I should learn," said Babette; "for he greatly desired that I should read the New Testament."

"Frollo, what would you say if you heard the new printing-presses were likely to send forth a New Testament in the French language?" said Farel, quickly.

"I would say, if this could be so, and the people would learn to read it for themselves, that the gospel need not fear the frown even of our puissant monarch, King Francis," replied the armorer. But the next minute he shook his head. "You will have to keep on with your Latin," he said, speaking to Babette; "the Church would never allow this, that the people should read the Scriptures in their own tongue."

"But our little professor of the Sorbonne is determined that they shall have it," said Farel; "he will himself translate the gospels as soon as he has time at command; and the noble and gentle Monsieur Berquin has already commenced the translation of several Christian books into French."

"Nay, nay, that cannot be. Your pardon, Monsieur Farel; but this Berquin, a gentlemen of Artois, is a customer of my own, and many times have I heard him speak of the veneration he felt for all the doctrines and ordinances of the Church."

Farel smiled. "That was before the syndic, Bedier, made such an outcry against the Scriptures,"

PUISSANT: *powerful*

he said; "his violent declamation against God's Word has raised in many minds a desire to read it; and Berquin has done so, with the same result as Gérard Roussel, and so many others. He has embraced the gospel, and determined to make it known to others, by translating Christian books into the language of the people."

"And these same books—how are the people to get them?" asked Claude, eagerly.

It was a difficulty unforeseen by Dr. Farel. Those were not the days of bookselling as a trade; and only in a few cities like Paris had the art of printing been heard of as yet. Claude noticed the look of perplexity in the doctor's face, and his own brightened.

"Let me have some of these same books to sell," he said. "I could take some wares as a peddler; and while I showed my strips of taffetas and other braveries, I could likewise bring forth my books, and speak a word to the people on the love of God."

Madame and Babette both laughed at the idea of Claude selling taffetas and finery; but Dr. Farel by no means derided the idea. He begged Claude to stay at Meaux for a few days before setting out on his journey to Dauphiny; for the ex-monk had decided that the first use he would make of his liberty should be to go and see his mother.

DERIDED: *ridiculed*

Chapter XVI

The Peddler

DURING the several months which passed ere we again take up the thread of our story, important events were happening in the history of the Reformation in France. The brief visit of King Francis to his capital, by which the armorer's life was saved, was only the signal for a powerful resistance to be made to the noted Concordat; and while the king passed his time in tilting matches, hunting parties, and tournaments, the University and Parliament were trying to throw off the despotic yoke by which their young king sought to bind them. But all in vain. The queen-mother and her party were too powerful; and just as Farel had foreseen, ignorance and fanaticism joined hands at last with profligacy and corruption, and together they agreed to quench the newly-arisen light in which so many had learned to rejoice.

But meanwhile, Lefèvre, Farel, and Roussel were still preaching as earnestly as ever; and the noble

Berquin was translating his books. After numerous delays, Farel had contrived to send some of these to Meaux, where his friends had settled in the clothworking quarter of the city, and among some relatives of Claude's, who had promised to protect him should any violence be attempted by the monks.

His peddler's pack was soon prepared; and when, at length, the tractates arrived from the Paris printing-presses, he set off on his long journey to Dauphiny.

His journey occupied him some weeks, for anxious as he was to reach his native village once more, he never lost an opportunity of reading something from the books he carried, and telling the wonderful news of God's free salvation. Peddlers were very important people in those days. Their coming to a village was hailed almost as a holiday, and people gathered round to hear the news of what was going on in the great world beyond the forests which generally encircled them. Letters and messages for friends and relatives were often committed to the peddler's hands. Thus they were trusted with many secrets, and respected accordingly.

Claude had not sold all his books, when at length the well-known vine slopes of his native village came in view; but a difficulty hitherto unthought of presented itself to his mind. Everybody here knew he had taken the vows of a priest, and what would they say when they saw him carrying

TRACTATES: *tracts, essays*

a peddler's pack? His mother and sisters, too, had to be considered; for the disgrace that had fallen upon him in being degraded from his office would inevitably fall upon them, and the cry of "heretic" would be raised the moment he was recognized.

Undecided what course to adopt for the best, Claude sat down on the road leading from Grenoble; and placing his pack beside him, he bowed his head in his hands, and lifted up his heart to God in earnest prayer for guidance and protection. When he lifted his head a girl stood before him, and in a moment he had sprung to his feet, exclaiming, "Margot, Margot! do you not know me?"

But the girl stepped back frowning. "My name is not Margot," she said; "my name is Fanchon."

Claude recollected himself in time not to follow the girl, although it was his sister, for he saw that she did not recognize him. "Your pardon, Mademoiselle," he said, speaking as calmly as he could; "but I knew someone in Paris a few years ago who was greatly like you."

"My sister has been to Paris, and so have I," said the girl, tossing her head with an air of importance; "and I have a brother there now," she added. "Perhaps you bring us tidings of him," she suddenly exclaimed; "I will go and call my sister Margot;" and she was speeding off, without waiting to hear the peddler's reply.

But Claude called her back. "It is not meet that your sister should come out to see a poor peddler.

I will come to her; and, it may be, can let her have a bargain in cloth or taffetas, or even a book, besides bringing news of your brother Claude."

"How did you know his name was Claude?" said Fanchon, quickly. "He is a holy monk now, and people call him Father Augustine."

Claude saw that he had betrayed himself; but, without noticing the girl's words, he said: "And your mother and sister, are they quite well? Your brother is very anxious to know everything concerning them."

"Margot is quite well. She is married, you know; but mother is very ill—so ill that 'tis feared she will never get better," said Fanchon, with a sigh.

Claude quickened his pace. "Will you point me the way to your mother's cottage," he said, looking at the same moment in the direction of his old home.

Fanchon noticed the look. "We used to live in that cottage," she said; "but when we came back from Paris, Margot was married to Maître Pierre Martel, and now we live with her."

Claude remembered where Martel's cottage used to stand, and pressed on eagerly. At the corner of the garden, evidently looking for Fanchon, stood his sister Margot; and she looked surprised and not quite pleased to see her sister talking to this strange peddler. The fact was, Fanchon had been spoilt by that visit to Paris. She gave herself airs, and considered herself superior now to all her village friends; and, moreover, she had been so greatly indulged by her mother lately, that the girl's ways and manners often caused her sister great anxiety.

She was looking very much displeased now. "Fanchon, how could you leave—"

But Fanchon hastily interrupted her. "Don't be angry now, Margot," she said. "This peddler has come from Paris to bring us news of Claude."

Margot looked at the peddler. "Have you seen my brother lately?" she said, for a faint rumor of his disgrace had reached her through a neighbor. Fanchon, however, knew nothing of this, and tossed her head the higher when talking of "my brother, Father Augustine."

Claude could scarcely repress the impulse to clasp his beloved sister in his arms; but he managed to bow in answer to her question, and follow her calmly up the garden path into the cottage.

The moment the door closed, however, he threw down his pack, pushed aside the slouching cap that half-covered his face, and with a low cry, "Margot! Margot! my dear sister Margot! do you not know me?" he clasped his sister in his arms.

Margot turned pale, and staggered from his encircling arms as soon as she could. "Claude," she gasped, "it cannot be my brother Claude." The voice was one of such intense horror that Claude could only cover his face with his hands, and groan aloud. His head still bore the marks of the clerical tonsure, although his hair was beginning to grow; but it was enough to convince Margot that it was indeed her brother standing before her, in the disguise of a peddler.

For a minute or two neither could speak again; but at length Claude managed to say, "My mother, Margot, may I see her?"

Another fit of shuddering horror seized Margot at the mention of her mother. "Claude, it will kill her to see you thus," she said, in a faint whisper. "Pierre heard from a neighbor who had been to Paris that you had been degraded; but oh, to leave the monastery thus," and Margot put her hands to her eyes, as though she would shut out the sight of her brother's face.

Poor Claude! He had not thought that his dearly-loved sister, his gentle Margot, would receive him thus, and the sudden shock quite overcame him. He sank down upon the floor with a faint moan, not quite insensible, but sick with the dreadful faintness that had seized him more than once since that night of horrible suffering and torture he had passed in the monastery. Margot was at his side in a moment.

"Oh, Claude, Claude," she sobbed, raising his head and kissing him in her passion and grief and sorrow; "Oh, Claude, only look up, and speak to me once more."

Fanchon had rushed from the room as Claude entered it to tell her mother that news had been brought from Paris by the peddler; and she now came back to ask him to go and see the invalid, so that she knew nothing of the disclosure that had been made, and was not a little surprised to see and hear what she did.

"What is it?—what has happened?" she managed to say at length, looking down at the prostrate figure on the floor.

"Oh, Fanchon, I have killed him—killed our brother Claude," gasped Marguerite.

Fanchon stepped back aghast. "Claude!" she repeated, "that man is not our brother Claude."

"Hush, hush, Fanchon! Mother must not hear of it yet. Run back, and tell her he is too tired to come and see her just now, and bring me some of the wine that Madame Farel sent from the château."

Fanchon slowly went on her errand, still staring with horror at the prostrate figure, feeling sure and yet dreading to hear that it was indeed her brother Claude.

When she came back with the wine, Marguerite poured a little into a drinking horn, and again taking her brother's head on her arm, put it to his lips; and when she found he had swallowed a little, she kissed him again and again in a rapture of delight. "Now one little drop more," she said, coaxingly, as she again put the horn to his lips, and Claude managed to take a "little drop more," and then slowly opened his eyes, and tried to get up. But Marguerite would not allow this.

She still knelt at his side, supporting his head on her shoulder. At last he managed to say, "I am better now. This faintness has seized me several times since—" and then he stopped with a shudder.

"Since when?" asked Marguerite, tenderly.

But Claude shook his head. Not yet could he tell that tale of horror. "By and by, when I feel stronger it shall be told," he whispered. "But now, Margot, kiss me again, and tell me you forgive me."

Marguerite kissed the worn face; but before she could speak Fanchon said, "If you are our brother Claude, you seem sadly to have forgotten the disgrace you have brought upon us."

"Hush, hush, we can bear the disgrace," said Marguerite, quickly. All her affection had been appealed to by her brother's helpless state, and she would not think of anything else just now.

Claude looked at Fanchon, and sighed deeply. He could not say anything just now; but when she moved aside, and Marguerite took one of his long bony hands in hers, he whispered, "Have you forgotten 'David's Royal Fountain,' my Margot?"

Marguerite shook her head. "I could never forget what I heard while with you in Paris," she said. "Mother, too, has given up praying to the Virgin, and prays only to the Lord Christ."

"Then, Margot, will the disgrace be very hard to bear when it is for His dear sake?" said Claude, in a low tone.

Marguerite, however, still clung to the old superstitions, in spite of the light that had dawned upon her soul, and she said, rather quickly, "But, Claude, you could have been a more true and holy monk through the knowledge of Christ the Lord."

"Yes; but I must needs tell others of the one atonement for sin—that neither priest nor pope can forgive sins, but only the Lord Christ Himself," said Claude, earnestly.

Marguerite bowed her head. "And you did this, my brother?" she said, softly.

"Yes; and was accused of teaching strange doctrines, and a cry of heresy was raised against me; and because I refused to give up my belief in them I was put to the torture, and deprived of all my offices."

A low cry escaped Marguerite's lips. "The torture?" she repeated.

"Yes, yes; I cannot speak more of it now," said Claude; "it was feared I should ever be a cripple through the severity of it, but God released me from that fear, and through the kindness of the king's physician 'tis only my arms and hands that continue weak."

Fanchon had drawn nearer while her brother was speaking. "Who was it put you to the torture?" she asked; "were you sent to prison?"

Claude shook his head. "'Twas in the monastery I suffered, and by the prior's order," he said. "But enough of this, my sister," he added; "let me go to my mother now. Marguerite, will you prepare her for my coming?" he said, slowly raising himself from his sister's supporting arms.

She glanced at his half-crippled hands, and the last remnant of her anger died out. "My brother, forgive me," she said; "we will share your disgrace without murmuring. Fanchon, bring Claude a little more wine, while I go to Mother."

Claude tried to make his peace with his younger sister while Marguerite was gone; but Fanchon was too much offended—the disgrace of having a degraded monk for a brother was too much for her pride, and she turned away, after giving him the wine, without answering his question.

In a minute or two, Marguerite came back. "You will be patient with Mother?" she said, as she led him from the room.

"Margot, that were a needless question," he said; and as he reached his mother's bedside, he fell upon his knees, and bowed his head to receive her blessing.

This action seemed to bring to her mind more forcibly than anything else could have done, the change in her son's condition. She extended her hands, but murmured, "Oh, Claude, my son, my son, you should be blessing me; and I had hoped you would perform masses for my soul after I had gone to the grave." There was no anger in her voice, but such a depth of sorrow and sadness that touched Claude much more keenly.

"Oh, my mother," he murmured, kissing her hands, but not attempting to rise; "Oh, my mother, forgive your unhappy Claude."

"I forgive you, Claude," murmured the widow; "but, oh, it is a cruel blow. I had hoped so much from your being a priest, that God would accept—"

"Mother, Mother, it will make no difference whether I am a priest or not. God will receive all who come to Him in the name of the Lord Christ," interrupted Claude.

"Yes, yes; I know if they can live a holy, religious life; but I never could, my son. I had the vineyard to think of, and the goats' milk to look after, or else you would have starved: and so it was in mercy I came to Paris, and learnt that 'the blood of Jesus Christ cleanseth us from all sin,' without poor people having to pay for it."

"And, my mother, do you not think the Lord Christ would pardon your sin, even though your life had to be spent in the performance of every-day duties?" said Claude.

"But, my son, I gave you up to the service of the Church, just when you could have helped me in the vineyard. Surely there was some merit in that," added the widow.

Claude shook his head. "My mother, the Lord Christ saves us freely, without any merit of our own, or that of friends," he said.

But the widow looked up quickly. "I have not heard yet how you came to leave the monastery," she said, in a stern tone.

The Last Meeting and Parting

Claude sat down at her side, and related all the circumstances, passing lightly over what he had suffered at the hands of his brother monks; but this evidently made a deep impression on his mother's mind, for she took his hand in hers, murmuring, "My poor boy, my poor Claude, how much you have suffered!"

Chapter XVII

Conclusion

"MY son, what is this year?" The speaker was the widow Leclerc, and she turned restlessly towards Claude as she spoke.

He looked as though he did not quite understand her meaning, and she repeated her question. "How long is it since you left home to go to Paris?" she added; "I could always tell until lately, but my memory is failing now," she sighed.

"Nine years," replied Claude; "I left in 1510, and now it is 1519. Mother," he suddenly added, "they have been nine wonderful years, not only for France, but for Germany and Switzerland; and it is even hoped that our foes the English will share in the blessing God is now giving to the nations of Europe."

"What blessing?" asked the invalid.

"Mother, can you ask?" exclaimed Claude. "Nay, nay; now you have learned to trust in the Lord Christ, and rejoice in the free grace proclaimed in God's Word, can you think anything of worth

besides this; and it is indeed a matter of rejoicing
that though our beloved land, as the most favored
of all nations, was the first to receive the light of
this gospel, others are receiving it likewise. Not
long ago, in Germany, a humble monk began to
declare to the people that sin could not be pardoned by the purchase of the pope's indulgences;
that the blood of Christ alone could take away sin;
and what our noble professor of the Sorbonne, Dr.
Lefèvre, began to preach and lecture about seven
years ago, Martin Luther is preaching now at his
University of Wittenberg."

The widow, in spite of the disappointment she
felt at Claude's being degraded from his priestly
office, loved to hear him talk of things above the
general comprehension of her neighbors, although
it may be doubted whether she herself understood
much more about it than they would. But it was
enough for her that he did; and so she listened
with the greatest attention, and often asked some
question to show that she was trying to compre-
hend it all. So she now said, "And this doctrine is
spreading to other countries, my son?"

"Yes, Mother; just across the mountains in Switzerland, one Ulric Zwingle, a priest, began to
preach this same doctrine three years ago, at the
Abbey Church of 'Our Lady of the Hermitage.'
'Twas a grand place of pilgrimage, wonderful as
our own St. Croix; for over the gate was written, 'In
this place is to be found a full remission of all sins.'

And here Zwingle taught that it was not pilgrimages, or indulgences, or the Virgin, that could take away sin; but only the precious blood of the Lord Christ. Mother, I wish someone at our St. Croix would preach this true and life-giving doctrine," added Claude, earnestly.

"My son, do not speak of St. Croix," said the widow; "I would fain forget it now, though at one time I thought it would be a comfort on my deathbed to think of the pilgrimages I had taken thither."

"But, Mother, why should you dread to think of it so much?" asked Claude. "We know that these idols are but lying vanities, and the miracles they talk of are but contrivances of the priests."

"Hush, hush, my son; speak not rashly of these things, for you know not what power they may possess," said the widow, in an imploring whisper. She could not divest herself entirely of her belief in the power of these things, although she had given up her faith in them as the means of salvation.

"But, Mother, God has given all men reason, and desires them to use it in His service; and to each He has likewise given a conscience, not merely to those who are priests, that they may be the conscience for others."

"My son," interrupted the widow, "I cannot understand all this. I am not learned. I only know that the Church used to decide what was right and wrong; and it seems as though the world were coming to an end that it is not so now; but, of course,

DIVEST: *free*

you know best—you and Dr. Farel at the Sorbonne and all the other great people at Paris."

Claude kissed the wan, pallid face, and went out in search of Marguerite, whom he sent to his mother; while he went to a little loft at the back of the house, where he knew he should be secure from interruption; for he longed to pour out his soul in thankfulness to God that his mother had been enabled in some degree to grasp the hope of salvation.

The object of his journey Claude felt was now accomplished. But he had no intention of returning yet, although his stay here was not too pleasant. The news of his degradation had reached the neighbors, who were not slow in letting the family know it, and which Fanchon resented accordingly, not only to the neighbors but to her brother and sister as well. She reproached Marguerite for encouraging this lengthened stay, and her brother for coming to disgrace them in the eyes of all the village. Marguerite took the reproaches meekly enough. Fanchon, however, fretted and fumed, and reproached first her brother, and then Marguerite, openly wishing he would shoulder his peddler's pack again, and depart from Dauphiny.

The departure came sooner than she expected; but it was preceded by another that for a time broke down all her pride, and made her forget her angry reproaches. The life of the widow had well-nigh come to an end when she had the

PALLID: *pale*

conversation with her son just reported; and a few days afterwards she departed to that land where the inhabitants say no more, "I am sick."

Claude would fain have stayed and seen his mother laid in the grave but Marguerite and Pierre begged him to hasten his departure. They feared lest some of the villagers, who were more than ordinarily angry with him for the supposed disgrace he had brought upon their native place, would create a disturbance, and have driven him out by force, now that the widow was dead.

For his sister's sake, therefore—to spare her the unpleasant consequences of such a disturbance— Claude determined to leave the following night; and, taking the road leading to Gap, make his way back to Meaux by a different route from that which he had taken in coming to Dauphiny.

It was a sad and tender parting between the brother and sister—the more sad on account of their recent loss, and the uncertainty whether they should ever meet again until they met before the throne of God. It would be hardly safe for Claude to venture there again, even if he came with his pack into the neighborhood. But he promised to let Marguerite hear of his welfare, from time to time, through the Farel family. He likewise promised that when Dr. Lefèvre fulfilled his promise, and gave to the people a New Testament in their own tongue, one of the first copies should be sent to Marguerite. Begging she would make this Book the guide and rule of her life, he departed once more for the north.

Claude reached Meaux in safety, after an absence of several months, and found his friends very comfortably settled in their new home. It was of course different from the one they had been driven from in Paris. But Frollo was becoming reconciled to his change of position, and making himself useful, not only as a diligent and skillful worker at his trade, but among his neighbors he was making known those glorious, life-giving truths for which he had suffered; and none listened to him with more devout attention than young Leclerc, the woolcomber, Claude's kinsman. His father and the rest of his family were most devoted in their adherence to the Church; but this did not prevent the young woolcomber from listening to the teaching of Claude and the armorer. The fact that they had had to suffer loss for this gospel only drew him the more strongly towards it and he felt that he too would gladly suffer the loss of all things to spread the knowledge of Christ, and the free salvation He has perfected.

Little did he think, as he said this, that in a few short years he would be called upon to prove his constancy in this same city of Meaux—that he would be publicly and shamefully beaten through its streets, and finally branded in the forehead as a heretic; and yet that his faith should be strengthened by the firmness of his mother, who encouraged him to endure all this suffering and torment, until the last supreme moment of agony, when she saw the red-hot branding iron applied to his forehead, and the streets rang with her agonized shrieks. It was a fierce contest between faith and natural affection; but faith gained the victory. Looking at her brave, intrepid martyr-son, she exclaimed, in a loud voice, "Glory to Jesus Christ, and to His witnesses."[1] As yet, however, no one interfered with these humble, faithful witnesses, laboring in the clothworking quarter of the city.

Soon after his return, Claude and Babette were married in a quiet, simple fashion. To earn a living for himself and his wife, he went out into the surrounding districts with his pack of cloth and taffetas, knives and books. In a village to the south of Meaux, he one day met a Franciscan monk of Avignon, and, to his astonishment, heard him preach the very same doctrines as he had learned from the doctors of the Sorbonne.

Claude's astonishment was only equaled by his delight; and he eagerly pressed through the crowd, when the monk had finished his sermon, and begged to know where he had learned these doctrines.

Brother Francis smiled, and drew from his breast a few tattered leaves of a book. "The rest was taken from me and burnt," he said; "but I managed to save these. The book is written by one Martin

[1] D'Aubigné's *History of the Reformation*
INTREPID: *fearless*
LEAVES: *pages*

Luther, a German monk, and was bought at the Lyons fair."

Claude opened his pack. "I, too, have books to sell, written in our own tongue, teaching these same truths. Go on, my brother, for it is the truth of God, and must conquer all the powers of evil. As our noble professor of the Sorbonne saith, 'God is about to renew the world, and He will do it by His Word—by giving to the people the uncorrupted Word of God.'"

Brother Francis, however, was not so sanguine as Claude. He shook his head sadly as he said, "Ah, my brother, but there will be many a battle fought and lost in this France before the victory is gained. This book of mine was burned, and I have been persecuted for holding the truth it teaches—the truth that has set me free."

"But the Sorbonne is even now considering this matter—whether this Luther is a heretic or not," said Claude, quickly.

"And you will think him a heretic if he is condemned," said brother Francis.

"Nay, nay, I know he teaches the truth of God; for I, too, have read some of his tracts, and have heard much concerning him; and I would say there is hope that his works may be approved by the University, and disseminated among the people."

This strongly expressed hope of Claude's was, however, doomed to a speedy downfall. Shortly after he returned home to Meaux, he heard that a few days previously Luther's works had been publicly burnt at Paris, and the Sorbonne had decreed that he should retract all that he had written.

It was a heavy blow to the little body of Christians gathered at Meaux, when they heard the news, for they felt sure it was but the first step— that the whole power of the Church was rising in a resolve to crush out the new life that had sprung up in her midst. Anxiously did the armorer question every chance traveler from Paris, in order to know what was passing there: whether King Francis would allow his friends to be silenced by their enemies.

Little, however, could be learned beyond the fact that the king was making a progress through the kingdom, and giving himself up wholly to the indulgence of pleasure, which he could not do so freely when under the observation of the citizens of Paris, and these same friends of the Sorbonne.

The news from Paris, instead of deterring Claude from selling the books he obtained from the new printing-presses, only stirred him up to more diligence in the work. He foresaw that a time would come when he might not have the power he now had to go among the people; not only selling his books and wares, but likewise teaching and preaching the truth—and so he wisely made the most of his present opportunity.

PROGRESS: *journey*

As many feared, the condemnation of Luther and his works, was only the prelude to an attack upon Lefèvre and the Sorbonne doctors. The syndic and his adherents, the monks and priests, made sure they would be successful this time. Once before they had obtained his condemnation upon a point that then roused all Christendom. Lefèvre had asserted that Mary, the sister of Lazarus, Mary Magdalene, and "the woman which was a sinner," mentioned by St. Luke, were three distinct persons. The Church then held that they were one person; and so widely did the news of this *heresy* of Lefèvre spread, that Fisher, bishop of Rochester, wrote against him; and Bedier made sure he would see the noble old man end his days on the scaffold for preaching it.

But King Francis rescued him from the power of his enemies, as he had previously rescued Frollo; and, for a time, the professor had a little peace. Now, however, that Luther had been condemned, and King Francis was occupied with hunting, tilting, and tournaments, they resolved upon a second attack. But again the king interposed. "I will not have these people molested," he said; "to persecute those who teach us would prevent able scholars from coming into our country." Learning was all Francis cared for, but this he would protect; and, moreover, he was rather pleased to be able to humble the University that had opposed his Concordat, and prove that his boast was not an idle

INTERPOSED: *intervened*

one—that he had put the kings of France out of
leading strings.

But although they failed either to silence Lefèvre,
or bring him to the scaffold, they did not cease
their persecutions. Failing to seize the shepherd,
they did not fail to worry and torment the sheep
of the flock; and many a humble citizen of Paris,
who had embraced the truth, now took refuge in
Meaux; for it was well-known that Briçonnet, the
bishop of this diocese, was very favorably disposed
towards the new opinions.

Thus Paris drove from her midst this glorious
gospel, and brought upon herself the judgments
of God; for "this is the condemnation, that light
is come into the world, and men loved darkness
rather than light, because their deeds were evil."[1]

Amidst many things which continued to distress
and discourage our friends at Meaux, one circum-
stance inspired them with hope and confidence.
This was the translation of the New Testament.
The autumn of the year 1522 saw this work completed. In October, Claude went forth—his pack
laden with copies of the Four Gospels in French;
and after a month's absence he returned to find
that the remaining books of the New Testament
were ready.

The armorer scarcely knew how to restrain his
joy when he saw the books, and heard Babette
read from them in their own tongue the wonderful words of salvation.

[1] JOHN 3:19
LEADING STRINGS: *strings used to support a child learning
to walk*

"My child, it is enough," he said, laying his hand on the young matron's head; "I can go home to God now, and believe He will renew the world, though Dr. Lefèvre should die, and Dr. Farel be driven from France; for now that the people can have the Scriptures in their own tongue, they can themselves judge whether the Church teaches truth or error."

"The Church *must* teach the truth now," said Claude; "'David's Royal Fountain' is no longer hidden, but men may come and drink of it freely, now that God's Word is sent forth to reveal it. I would not be other than I am— a humble peddler making known this Word—no, not for the throne of King Francis."

*   *   *

And here we must take leave of our friends at Meaux, echoing, as our wish and prayer, the words of our hero—that the truth may yet be victorious in France, although the battle often seems a doubtful one. The story of the suppression of her Reformation is written in blood and tears; and the unhappy country is still paying the fearful price of the choice she made three hundred years ago— darkness, when light was offered; error, when truth was proclaimed; and among her countless martyrs were many who were "faithful, though not famous."

The End

ABOUT THE AUTHOR

Emma Leslie (1837-1909), whose actual name was Emma Dixon, lived in Lewisham, Kent, in the south of England. She was a prolific Victorian children's author who wrote over 100 books. Emma Leslie's first book, *The Two Orphans*, was published in 1863 and her books remained in print for years after her death. She is buried at the St. Mary's Parish Church, in Pwllcrochan, Pembroke, South Wales.

Emma Leslie brought a strong Christian emphasis into her writing and many of her books were published by the Religious Tract Society. Her extensive historical fiction works covered many important periods in church history. Her writing also included a short booklet on the life of Queen Victoria published in the 50th year of the Queen's reign.

GLAUCIA THE GREEK SLAVE
A Tale of Athens in the First Century

After the death of her father, Glaucia is sold to a wealthy Roman family to pay his debts. She tries hard to adjust to her new life but longs to find a God who can love even a slave. Meanwhile, her brother, Laon, struggles to find her and to earn enough money to buy her freedom. But what is the mystery that surrounds their mother's disappearance years earlier and will they ever be able to read the message in the parchments she left for them?

THE CAPTIVES
Or, Escape from the Druid Council

The Druid priests are as cold and cruel as the forest spirits they claim to represent, and Guntra, the chief of her tribe of Britons, must make a desperate deal with them to protect those she loves. Unaware of Guntra's struggles, Jugurtha, her son, longs to drive the hated Roman conquerors from the land. When he encounters the Christian centurion, Marcinius, Jugurtha mocks the idea of a God of love and kindness, but there comes a day when he is in need of love and kindness for himself and his beloved little sister. Will he allow Marcinius to help him? And will the gospel of Jesus Christ ever penetrate the brutal religion of the proud Britons?

www.SalemRidgePress.com

OUT OF THE MOUTH OF THE LION
Or, The Church in the Catacombs

When Flaminius, a high Roman official, takes his wife, Flavia, to the Colosseum to see Christians thrown to the lions, he has no idea the effect it will have. Flavia cannot forget the faith of the martyrs, and finally, to protect her from complete disgrace or even danger, Flaminius requests a transfer to a more remote government post. As he and his family travel to the seven cities of Asia Minor mentioned in Revelation, he sees the various responses of the churches to persecution. His attitude toward the despised Christians begins to change, but does he dare forsake the gods of Rome and embrace the Lord Jesus Christ?

SOWING BESIDE ALL WATERS
A Tale of the World in the Church

There is newfound freedom from persecution for Christians under the emperor, Constantine, but newfound troubles as well. Errors and pagan ways are creeping into the Church, while many of the most devoted Christians are withdrawing from the world into the desert as hermits and nuns. Quadratus, one of the emperor's special guards, is concerned over these developments, even in his own family. Then a riot sweeps through the city and Quadratus' home is ransacked. When he regains consciousness, he finds that his sister, Placidia, is gone. Where is she? And can the Church handle the new freedom, and remain faithful?

www.SalemRidgePress.com

Emma Leslie Church History Series

FROM BONDAGE TO FREEDOM
A Tale of the Times of Mohammed

At a Syrian market two Christian women are sold as slaves. One of the slaves ends up in Rome where Bishop Gregory is teaching his new doctrine of "purgatory" and the need for Christians to finish paying for their own sins. The other slave travels with her new master, Mohammed, back to Arabia, where Mohammed eventually declares himself to be the prophet of God. In Rome and Arabia, the two women and countless others fall into the bondage of man-made religions—will they learn at last to find true freedom in the Lord Jesus Christ alone?

THE MARTYR'S VICTORY
A Story of Danish England

Knowing full well they may die in the attempt, a small band of monks sets out to convert the savage Danes who have laid waste to the surrounding countryside year after year. The monks' faith is sorely tested as they face opposition from the angry Priest of Odin as well as doubts, sickness and starvation, but their leader, Osric, is unwavering in his attempts to share the "White Christ" with those who reject Him. Then the monks discover a young Christian woman who has escaped being sacrificed to the Danish gods—can she help reach those who had enslaved her and tried to kill her?

GYTHA'S MESSAGE
A Tale of Saxon England

Having discovered God's love for her, Gytha, a young slave, longs to escape the violence and cruelty of the world and devote herself to learning more about this God of love. Instead she lives in a Saxon household that despises the name of Christ. Her simple faith and devoted service bring hope and purpose to those around her, especially during the dark days when England is defeated by William the Conqueror. Through all of her trials, can Gytha learn to trust that God often has greater work for us to do *in* the world than *out* of it?

www.SalemRidgePress.com

EMMA LESLIE CHURCH HISTORY SERIES

LEOFWINE THE MONK
Or, The Curse of the Ericsons
A Story of a Saxon Family

Leofwine, unlike his wild, younger brother, finds no pleasure in terrorizing the countryside, and longs to enter a monastery. Shortly after he does, however, he hears strange rumors of a monk who preaches "heresy". Unable to stop thinking about these new ideas, Leofwine at last determines to leave the monastery and England. Leofwine's search for inner peace takes him to France and Rome and finally to Jerusalem, but in his travels, he uncovers a plot against his beloved country. Will he be able to help save England? And will he ever find true rest for his troubled soul?

ELFREDA THE SAXON
Or, The Orphan of Jerusalem
A Sequel to Leofwine

When Jerusalem is captured by the Muslims, Elfreda, a young orphan, is sent back to England to her mother's sister. Her aunt is not at all pleased to see her, and her uncle fears she may have brought the family curse back to England. Elfreda's cousin, Guy, who is joining King Richard's Crusade, promises Elfreda that he will win such honor as a crusader that the curse will be removed. Over the years that follow, however, severe trials befall the family and Guy and Elfreda despair of the curse ever being lifted. Is it possible that there is One with power stronger than any curse?

DEARER THAN LIFE
A Story of the Times of Wycliffe

When a neighboring monastery lays claim to one of his fields, Sir Hugh Middleton refuses to yield his property, and further offends the monastery by sending his younger son, Stephen, to study under Dr. John Wycliffe. At the same time, Sir Hugh sends his elder son, Harry, to serve as an attendant to the powerful Duke of Lancaster. As Wycliffe seeks to share the Word of God with the common people, Stephen and Harry and their sisters help spread the truth, but what will it cost them in the dangerous day in which they live?

www.SalemRidgePress.com

EMMA LESLIE CHURCH HISTORY SERIES

BEFORE THE DAWN
A Tale of Wycliffe and Huss

To please her crippled grandson, Conrad, Dame Ursula allows a kindly blacksmith and his friend, Ned Trueman, to visit the boy. Soon, however, she becomes suspicious that the men belong to the despised group who are followers of Dr. John Wycliffe, and she passionately warns Conrad of the dangers of evil "heresy". He decides to become a famous teacher in the Church so he can combat heresy, but he wonders why all the remedies of the Church fail to cure him. And why do his mother and grandmother refuse to speak of the father he has never known?

FAITHFUL, BUT NOT FAMOUS
A Tale of the French Reformation

Young Claude Leclerc travels to Paris to begin his training for the priesthood, but he is not sure *what* he believes about God. One day he learns the words to an old hymn and is drawn to the lines about "David's Royal Fountain" that will "purge every sin away." Claude yearns to find this fountain, and at last dares to ask the famous Dr. Lefèvre where he can find it. His question leads Dr. Lefèvre to set aside his study of the saints and study the Scriptures in earnest. As Dr. Lefèvre grasps the wonderful truth of salvation by grace, he wants to share it with Claude, but Claude has mysteriously disappeared. Where is he? And is France truly ready to receive the good news of the gospel of Jesus Christ?

www.SalemRidgePress.com

Church History for Younger Readers

SOLDIER FRITZ
A Story of the Reformation
by Emma Leslie
Illustrated by C. A. Ferrier

Young Fritz wants to follow in the footsteps of Martin Luther and be a soldier for the Lord, so he chooses a Bible from the peddler's pack as his birthday gift. When his father, the Count, goes off to war, however, Fritz and his mother and little sister are forced to flee into the forest to escape being thrown in prison for their new faith. Disguising themselves as commoners, they must trust the Lord as they wait and hope for the Count to rescue them. But how will he ever be able to find them?

www.SalemRidgePress.com

Fiction for Younger Readers

MARY JANE – HER BOOK
by Clara Ingram Judson
Illustrated by Francis White

This story, the first book in the Mary Jane series, recounts the happy, wholesome adventures of five-year-old Mary Jane and her family as she helps her mother around the house, goes on a picnic with the big girls, plants a garden with her father, learns to sew and more!

MARY JANE – HER VISIT
by Clara Ingram Judson
Illustrated by Francis White

In this story, the second book in the Mary Jane series, five-year-old Mary Jane has more happy, wholesome adventures, this time at her great-grandparents' farm in the country where she hunts for eggs, picks berries, finds baby rabbits, goes to the circus and more!

www.SalemRidgePress.com

Historical Fiction for Younger Readers

AMERICAN TWINS OF THE REVOLUTION
by Lucy Fitch Perkins

General Washington has no money to pay his discouraged troops and twins Sally and Roger are asked by their father, General Priestly, to help hide a shipment of gold which will be used to pay the American soldiers. Unfortunately, British spies have also learned about the gold and will stop at nothing to prevent it from reaching General Washington. Based on a true story, this is a thrilling episode from our nation's history!

MARIE'S HOME
Or, A Glimpse of the Past
by Caroline Austin
Illustrated by Gordon Browne R. I.

Eleven-year-old Marie Hamilton and her family travel to France at the invitation of Louis XVI, just before the start of the French Revolution. There they encounter the tremendous disparity between the proud French Nobility and the oppressed and starving French people. When an enraged mob storms the palace of Versailles, Marie and her family are rescued from grave danger by a strange twist of events, but Marie's story of courage, self-sacrifice and true nobility is not yet over! Honor, duty, compassion and forgiveness are all portrayed in this uplifting story.

www.SalemRidgePress.com

Historical Fiction by William W. Canfield

THE WHITE SENECA
Illustrated by G. A. Harker

Captured by the Senecas, fifteen-year-old Henry Cochrane grows to love the Indian ways and becomes Dundiswa—the White Seneca. When Henry is captured by an enemy tribe, however, he must make a desperate attempt to escape from them and rescue fellow captive, Constance Leonard. He will need all the skills he has learned from the Indians, as well as great courage and determination, if he is to succeed. But what will happen to the young woman if they do reach safety? And will he ever be able to return to his own people?

AT SENECA CASTLE
Illustrated by G. A. Harker

In this sequel to *The White Seneca*, Henry Cochrane, now eighteen, faces many perils as he serves as a scout for the Continental Army. General Washington is determined to do whatever it takes to stop the constant Indian attacks on the settlers and yet Henry is torn between his love for the Senecas and his loyalty to his own people. As the Army advances across New York State, Henry receives permission to travel ahead and warn his Indian friends of the coming destruction. But will he reach them in time? And what has happened to the beautiful Constance Leonard whom he had been forced to leave in captivity a year earlier?

THE SIGN ABOVE THE DOOR

Young Prince Martiesen is ruler of the land of Goshen in Egypt, where the Hebrews live. Eight plagues have already come upon Egypt and now Martiesen has been forced by Pharaoh to further increase the burden of the Hebrews. Martiesen, however, is in love with the beautiful Hebrew maiden, Elisheba, whom he is forbidden by Egyptian law to marry. As the nation despairs, the other nobles turn to Martiesen for leadership, but before he can decide what to do, Elisheba is kidnapped by the evil Peshala and terrifying darkness falls over the land. An exciting tale woven around the events of the Exodus from the Egyptian perspective!

www.SalemRidgePress.com

Adventure by George Manville Fenn

YUSSUF THE GUIDE
*Being the Strange Story of the Travels in Asia Minor of
Burne the Lawyer, Preston the Professor, and
Lawrence the Sick*
Illustrated by John Schönberg

    Young Lawrence, an invalid, convinces his guardians, Preston the Professor and Burne the Lawyer, to take him along on an archaeological expedition to Turkey. Before they set out, they engage Yussuf as their guide. Through the months that follow, the friends travel deeper and deeper into the remote regions of central Turkey on their trusty horses in search of ancient ruins. Yussuf proves his worth time and time again as they face dangers from a murderous ship captain, poisonous snakes, sheer precipices, bands of robbers and more. Memorable characters, humor and adventure abound in this exciting story!

www.SalemRidgePress.com

CPSIA information can be obtained at www.ICGtesting.com
Printed in the USA
LVOW051256181212

312177LV00001B/20/P

9 781934 671306